OPENING PANDORA'S BOX

BOOK FIVE: HOW CAN YOU DO THIS TO ME?

PETE ANDREWS

This is a work of fiction. ***All characters are of legal age and are 18 years old or older.***

First Edition. October 2023.

This book was written by and copyright © 2023 Pete Andrews. All rights reserved.

ABOUT THE AUTHOR

I write sexy romances. I used to publish under *xleglover* and *Flash of Stocking* on various sites.

My stories are romances, so they explore the feelings, emotions and relationships of the characters. My stories have an emotional edge to them. The characters have thrilling adventures, but there's pain there too, at least for some of them.

I try to write stories that seem like real life. Yes, the situations are extreme, but I hope you come away thinking, "*Yes, I can see how that might happened.*"

You can find my books at **Amazon Kindle** and **Smashwords**. Also, **Barnes & Noble, Apple Books,** and **Rakuten kobo**. If you'd like to join my mailing list or would like to send me a question or feedback, please email me at *peteandrews1701@gmail.com*.

BOOKS BY PETE ANDREWS

Faithful Wife's Fall From Grace (on-going series)

Book 1
Book 2
Book 3
Book 4

Girls Who Belong To Other Men (2 book series)

Book 1
Book 2

Opening Pandora's Box (5 book series)

Book 1: Jessie Plays For Her Husband
Book 2: Ollie Watches His Wife With Another Man
Book 3: Jessie Grows Closer To Roman
Book 4: Jessie Loses Herself In Roman
Book 5: How Can You Do This To Me?

Available at Amazon Kindle and Smashwords.

CHAPTER 1

After Ollie came, Jessie rose up onto her knees. As she did, she reached down and held the base of her husband's softening shaft to prevent the condom from slipping off.

She moved off Ollie, so she was on her knees next to him. She took off the condom and wrapped it in some tissues. Then she lowered her head and lovingly licked his penis clean.

After, Jessie snuggled into Ollie's arm. "This feels good," he said.

"Yeah," Jessie agreed.

"It feels weird. The way the short hair feels on my arm," Ollie said. "I'm used to feeling long hair."

Jessie rose up on an elbow and looked at her husband. "Do you still think I'm pretty?" she asked.

Ollie looked shocked at her question. "You look beautiful," he assured her. But seeing her short dark hair, he said, "You just look different."

Jessie pursed her lips. Then she glanced at the clock. "I should start getting ready," she said.

Ollie's insides began to churn. He knew she was talking about her date with Roman.

He nodded his head. Jessie gave him a weak smile, then moved from their bed to the bathroom.

Jessie showered, lathering her pussy multiple times. She brushed her teeth and swished mouthwash in her mouth. She knew Roman wouldn't want any evidence of Ollie on her body. She felt guilty, but at the same time, weak in her knees.

Jessie did her makeup the way Roman liked, heavier and darker. She looked better this way anyways, with the short dark hair.

She dressed in dark tones too. Little black dress and black stockings. Black heels. It fit her new look.

Also of course, underneath she had on one of the g-strings Roman gave her. And one of the garter belts. And she was braless.

Jessie went out to the TV room. Ollie was sipping a scotch. ESPN was on the TV, but it didn't seem like he was paying attention.

"How do I look?" Jessie asked. Ollie turned and looked at her.

"You look incredible," he said. He sounded sincere, but he didn't look happy. Especially as he looked at her face with the darker, heavier makeup, and the short dark hair.

Jessie didn't look like Ollie's wife anymore. She looked like Roman's girlfriend. And they both knew it. Ollie looked sad, but by this point, she knew his "angst" turned him on.

And Jessie knew how to push her husband's buttons. She took off her engagement ring and handed it to him for safekeeping. She wouldn't wear it again until she was back from her date with Roman.

Then Jessie took off her wedding ring from the ring finger of her left hand. "Can you hold this for me?" she asked Ollie. She gave her wedding ring to him.

Then Jessie took off Roman's #44 ring from her right hand, and put it on the ring finger of her left hand. She took her wedding ring from Ollie and put it on her right hand.

"How does it look?" she asked, holding up her left hand for Ollie to see Roman's ring on her wedding ring finger.

"I hate it," Ollie said, part serious, part joking.

Jessie smiled. She moved her left hand to Ollie's face. She ran the tip of her ring finger along his lips. "I think it gets you hot when I replace your wedding ring with Roman's ring," she said.

Ollie was suddenly breathing hard.

Jessie pushed her slender ring and middle fingers into Ollie's mouth. "Right?" she asked.

Ollie shook his head as he pulled away from her fingers. "No," he said.

Jessie grinned. She knew he was lying. "Anyways, I'm wearing your ring too," she said, referring to her wedding ring on her right hand.

"I thought it was our ring," Ollie said sourly.

"You know what I mean," Jessie said. Ollie scoffed but didn't push the issue.

"Are you happy he's exclusive to you?" Ollie asked.

"Yes," Jessie said honestly. "Just like you're exclusive to me. I'm not like you baby. I don't like sharing."

"You said he had threesomes with Alisha," Ollie said.

"Yeah?"

"What if he wants to do that with you?"

Jessie shook her head. "I don't share," she said.

"Not another girl," Ollie said. "Another man."

"I don't think Romes likes to share either," Jessie said.

"What about that taxi driver? Amir?"

Jessie shivered at the memory. "He wasn't sharing me," she said. "It was just a mind fuck."

"What if he wants to share you with Hammer?" Ollie asked.

Jessie's lips parted in surprise. She hadn't thought of that, as up to this point she associated Hammer with her new gig. Yet, she knew Roman and Hammer were close friends. And Roman said Hammer was wild.

"If Romes wants that, what do you think?" Jessie asked.

"Do I have any say in it?" Ollie asked.

Jessie considered a moment. "I guess not," she said. "He's my boyfriend, so I'll do what he wants me to do. Just like I do what you want me to do."

"Like how you cut and dyed your hair for Roman?" Ollie said.

"I did that for the part," Jessie insisted.

"So you're not excited to see Roman, to show him your new hair?"

"Okay, you're right," Jessie admitted. "What we're doing is crazy, right? I have you and Roman, and I'm trying to keep both of you happy. It's hard when you want different things."

"But I didn't do this for Romes," Jessie said, motioning to her hair. "I did it for the part."

Ollie nodded, but he didn't entirely believe her.

Jessie's phone dinged. She looked at the screen. It was a text from Roman.

"He's downstairs," Jessie said. "I guess I better get going."

Ollie nodded.

Jessie gave her husband a soft kiss to his lips. "I'll be back soon," she promised. With a crooked grin, she added "Then you can watch my boyfriend fuck my brains out."

CHAPTER 2

Jessie got into the taxi.

"Wait let me look at you," Roman said excitedly. He said to the driver "Can you turn on the light a second?"

Jessie looked warily at the driver. She was relieved to see it wasn't Amir.

"Fuck you look amazing!" Roman enthused admiringly, looking at Jessie with her short dark hair.

Jessie felt her heart flipping inside. She wanted to make him happy. And he was. So that made her happy.

"You're a real brunette now," he said, running his fingers through her hair. Her locks were still super soft, but not nearly as thick and lush as before. The stylist had severely thinned her hair so it had much less fullness and body. That's how Hammer wanted the dancers to look.

"You're better as a brunette than blonde," Roman said as he continued to look at her.

"I'm not sure about that," Jessie said with a laugh.

"No really. You're smoking hot Jessie. I mean you were before, but now ...," Roman said, his eyes still locked on her face. "I literally cannot take my eyes off you."

Jessie laughed again, and now she was blushing like a young schoolgirl. She *loved* making Roman happy. And the fact he thought she was so pretty and hot, that made her feel *soooo* good.

"How did Ollie like it?" Roman asked.

Jessie said, "He always supports me."

"He's your hero, right?" Roman said.

Jessie couldn't tell if he was being sarcastic or not. In any case, she answered, "He is."

Roman grinned and said, "Too bad he can't fuck you like I can." He said this in his normal voice, so the taxi driver could hear every world. Jessie shot him a warning look to lower his voice, but Roman ignored her.

"Okay, turn off the light and let's go," Roman told the driver. He tossed two fifties onto the front seat. "You can look back if you want, but don't drive off a bridge or anything. Okay?"

The driver was an older man, maybe in his 50s. He was thin and mostly bald. He didn't understand what Roman meant by "you can look back if you want." But seeing the money, he readily agreed. "Okay," the driver said. He began driving.

Once they were underway, Roman turned to Jessie and said, "Did you let your husband fuck you today?"

Roman was still speaking in his normal voice, so the driver could easily hear every word.

Jessie's eyes nervously glanced at the driver. He was looking at her in the rearview mirror. She looked back at Roman. "Yes," she whispered, her cheeks going red with embarrassment.

"And you made him wear a condom?"

"Yes," Jessie said in an even lower voice. She knew the driver was listening and stealing glances at her. She was so mortified.

Roman looked at the driver. "She's not on any birth control," he said. "So she makes her husband wear a condom. She doesn't want him to get her pregnant." Roman laughed. The driver smiled awkwardly.

"That's not true," Jessie whispered, her cheeks getting even redder. Too low for the driver to hear, but loud enough for Roman.

But Roman pretended not to hear her. He said, "And you're my little submissive slut, aren't you?"

Jessie nodded her head. She couldn't bear to answer aloud with the driver listening.

"Say it out loud Jessie," Roman ordered. He turned to the driver. "What's your name?"

"Jeff," the driver said. He was breathing hard. It was easy to tell he was turned on.

Roman turned back to Jessie. "Say it out loud so Jeff can hear you," he ordered. "Say, I'm your little submissive slut, and I'm cheating on my husband because your cock is bigger, and I make him wear condoms because I don't want him to get me pregnant."

Jessie looked down, not able to look at either Roman or Jeff. She said in a shaky voice that Jeff could hear, "I'm your little submissive slut. I'm cheating on Ollie. Because your cock is bigger than his."

"And you make Ollie wear a condom because you don't want him to get you pregnant," Roman pressed.

"You know that's not true," Jessie whispered.

Roman let it pass.

"I like that dress, Jessie. You look hot. Really hot," Roman said, abruptly changing the subject.

"Thank you," Jessie softly said. She didn't know what else to say. She certainly didn't feel charmed the way she'd felt moments ago when he was complimenting her.

"What are you wearing under the dress?" Roman said. They were stopped at a traffic light and Jeff was looking back at them. "Look at Jeff. Tell him what you're wearing under the dress," Roman ordered.

Jessie looked at Jeff. He was breathing even harder now, and the cheeks on his thin face were flushed with excitement. She instinctively knew he was hard, and maybe he was touching himself.

Looking into Jeff's eyes, Jessie said, "I'm wearing a g-string. And a garter belt. And black stockings."

"And?" Roman prompted. "Tell him what you're not wearing."

Feeling violated and humiliated, and still looking at Jeff, she softly whispered, "I'm not wearing a bra."

"Good girl," Roman said approvingly. "That's my little submissive slut."

Jessie was surprised when Roman began to work on his pants. He pulled them down, releasing his huge manhood. He was hard.

"Suck me off Jessie," Roman ordered her.

"Sir?" Jeff meekly said.

"Yeah Jeff?" Roman asked, looking at his new best friend.

"May I park over there, in that alley?" Jeff boldly asked. "And watch?"

Roman grinned. "Sure buddy, be my guest," he said.

Jeff quickly maneuvered the taxi into the alley. He parked next to an overhead light so the back of the taxi was illuminated.

"Go ahead Jessie," Roman said, looking into her eyes. "Suck my cock."

Jessie hesitated a moment. Then she lowered her head. She took his cock into her mouth.

"Yeah Jessie, that's it, just like that," Roman moaned, his eyes closing and his head rolling back.

Jessie had gotten better at sucking Roman. His cock was as huge as ever, but she had learned how he liked to be licked, stroked and sucked. She never tried to take him with just her mouth, the way she could with Ollie's cock. That wasn't possible given its immense size and heavy weight.

Even with her mouth wide open, she could barely swallow the big mushroom head and a couple inches of his shaft. Jessie used her hands to hold the part of his shaft not in her mouth, and even then, there were inches of his shaft not in either her mouth or hands. She had learned to stroke with her hands in sync with her head bobbing up and down, and he seemed to like it. He always said she gave good head.

Roman knew he wouldn't last long. Not with pretty Jessie's face buried in his crotch. She was the prettiest and sexiest girl he had ever met. Way hotter than Bianca or Fletcher, or the other girls at the gym. She blew away Alisha too, even on her best day back when she was younger and in her prime. And now she was even more stunning with the short dark hair. Any man will tell you a blow job is extra good when given by a really pretty girl.

Roman glanced over at Jeff. He was mostly hidden by the back of the front seats, but it was apparent the way his arm was moving that the old taxi driver was jerking off as he watched pretty Jessie blowing him.

Roman reached over Jessie and grabbed the bottom of her dress. He pulled it up, exposing her from the waist down. Fuck she looked hot in the g-string, garter belt and stockings!

Jeff's eyes went wide as he looked at Jessie's exposed ass and legs. He began jerking off more frantically.

"Go ahead and touch her if you want," Roman told him.

Jessie's body immediately stiffened, and she tried to pull away. Roman grabbed her hair and pinned her mouth on his cock. "If you fight, I'll let him fuck you," he threatened.

Jessie thought about her earlier conversation with Ollie, about whether Roman might want to share her with other men. She whined when she felt Jeff's hand on her ass.

Moments later, Roman came, shooting his jizz into Jessie's mouth. He held her head tight so she had no choice but to swallow. When he was finished, he let Jessie's head go. She rose up from his cock, gasping for air.

Roman glanced over at Jeff. From the way he was gasping, he had just cum too.

"Let's get going Jeff," Roman said as he pulled up his pants.

Jeff was still panting as he nodded to Roman. He pulled up his pants, sat back down in the driver's seat, and backed out of the alley.

Jessie's lips were wet, and her hair messed up. Despite that, she still looked incredibly beautiful and so smoking hot.

She began tugging down her dress but Roman stopped that. "Not yet Jessie," he said as he wrapped his arm around her shoulders, holding her so she couldn't squirm away. Then, with his other hand, he caressed her sensitive thighs above the stockings. He also caressed over the filmy material of the g-string covering her pussy.

Jessie stared at Roman as he caressed her. She was breathing hard, and aroused beyond belief. Her body was on fire and she wanted a cock inside her. She wanted Roman's cock inside her.

Roman knew he could get Jessie off in moments if he fingered her clit. He didn't do that. He edged her along, keeping her on the brink of an orgasm for the rest of the taxi ride, but denying her release.

"Why are you doing this to me?" Jessie asked helplessly. "Why won't you let me cum?"

"Do you want to let Ollie watch us later?" Roman asked.

"I told him he could," Jessie said.

"Your choice," Roman said. "Either I get you off, or we let Ollie watch us fuck."

"Romes ...," Jessie whined.

"Pick one," Roman told her. "You can't have both."

"I promised him," Jessie said.

"So that's your choice?"

"Make me cum," Jessie begged. "Please."

"Choose," Roman told her.

"He's my husband," Jessie said. "Watching is what he gets from this."

Roman shook his head. "Then you'll have to wait," he said as he pulled his hand away.

Feeling so sexually frustrated she wanted to scream, Jessie pulled her dress down.

CHAPTER 3

Roman took Jessie to *Per Se*, the famous Thomas Keller three-Michelin starred restaurant on Columbus Circle. Jessie was excited to go. She and Ollie had dined here once before, but it was too expensive for other than very special occasions. Jessie had begun to suspect Roman made more money than Ollie, and this was more evidence of that.

Jessie felt comfortable being with Roman in public. Her new short, dark hair and heavier make-up was a good disguise. She knew this disguise wouldn't last forever since it wasn't a disguise anymore, it was her new look, and people she knew would soon see her looking this way. But at least for this night she felt safe.

But her confidence was shattered when she heard someone calling her name. "Jessie? Is that you?" a woman asked, appearing at their table. The woman was with a man.

Jessie's heart sank. It was Stacy and her husband Simon! Simon worked with Ollie! "Oh god, this is a disaster!" she thought to herself.

"Oh ah, hi Stacy," Jessie sputtered. "Hi Simon."

"Jessie what have you done to your hair?" Stacy asked. She and Simon were both looking at her.

"I got a part on Broadway," Jessie explained, trying to keep the panic from her voice. Everyone knew it was her dream to dance on Broadway. "I mean, it's really off-Broadway, and a small part, but ... anyways, I had to change my hair for the part."

"Ollie must hate it," Stacy said. "You look good, but I know how much he's into blondes."

"Ollie supports me," Jessie said. Simon was staring at Roman.

Jessie had never liked Simon. He was one of those men who looked at her lips instead of her face whenever they spoke.

Stacy turned to look at Roman. "And you are?" she asked.

"This is Roman. He's my agent," Jessie quickly answered. She nervously sputtered, "We're, you know, celebrating my new part."

"I think I recognize you," Simon said to Roman. "You used to play for the Jets, right? And now you run that gym, Manhattan Motion?"

Jessie inwardly cursed. How the heck did Simon know that? Of all the millions of people who lived in New York City, freaking Simon knew about Roman with the Jets *and* Manhattan Motion? Really? How was that even possible? Jessie cursed her bad luck.

Roman smiled and smoothly said, "I'm trying to break into the business. I've got a few clients like Jessie I'm trying to help out."

"Ah, okay," Simon said, but he looked skeptical. "I've been to your place. Manhattan Motion. I've thought about joining."

Roman appraised Simon. "You look in good shape," he said.

Simon grinned at the compliment. "I'd like to get a bit more definition in my upper body," he said.

"Well, you look good already, but sure, stop by, I'll set you up," Roman said with a friendly smile. He was always open to new customers.

Simon then turned back to look at Jessie. She turned away so she didn't have to look him in the face. She always felt uncomfortable around Simon. When he looked at her, she always felt like he was undressing her in his head. More than once at work parties, he'd gotten in her space and even touched her. She thought he was an arrogant creep.

Stacy asked, "Where's Ollie? He's not celebrating with you?"

"Oh, well, you know, he's so busy at work," Jessie nervously sputtered. She was a terrible liar. "We celebrated last night."

"Okay, sure," Stacy said. She sounded as skeptical as her husband.

Simon was still looking at Jessie. His eyes were all over her. Jessie realized the little black dress she wore was too risqué for a celebratory dinner with her agent. Especially since Stacy and Simon could probably tell she was braless through the thin fabric of the dress.

And then with horror, Jessie remembered she wasn't wearing her engagement ring. And her wedding ring was on her right hand. She subtlety moved her hands to her lap under the tablecloth, hoping they hadn't noticed.

Once Simon and Stacy were gone, Jessie cringed as she lamented, "God this is terrible. Simon works with Ollie."

"I think they bought it," Roman said.

"You think so?" Jessie asked hopefully. "You don't think I'm dressed too racy for dinner with my agent?"

"Not if you're fucking your agent," Roman joked with a grin.

Jessie couldn't help grinning. And she knew Ollie got off on the mindfuck of people thinking she was cheating on him. With that thought, she tried to calm herself.

"Have you been here before?" Roman said, changing the subject.

"Just once. Ollie took me here when we moved to New York City. It was our anniversary too."

"So a special occasion," Roman said.

"It was," Jessie said.

"And did you have sex with Ollie that night?" he asked.

"It was years ago so I don't remember," Jessie said. "But probably. We always have sex on our anniversary."

"But not tonight," Roman said.

"No," Jessie said.

"I want to hear you say the words," Roman insisted.

"I'm not having sex with Ollie tonight," Jessie said. "I'm having sex with you." It was one of the rules. When she was with Roman, she was his girl, and Ollie was a platonic friend.

Grinning, Roman leaned closer and said, "I'm going to fuck you so good tonight, the next time Ollie takes you here, you'll think of me."

Jessie laughed. "You think so, huh?" she said, the laugh still in her voice.

"Maybe I'll finger you now," Roman said. "Get you off. Finish what I started in the taxi."

"I don't think so," Jessie said with another laugh. Simon and Stacy were at a table on the other side of the room. Far enough away they couldn't hear their conversation, but they could certainly see them.

"You were begging for it in the taxi," Roman said, grinning.

"You're crazy, you know that?" Jessie said with a nervous look over at Simon and Stacy.

"Take off your shoe, and put your foot in my lap," Roman told her. "I want you to feel how hard I am."

"You – are – freaking – crazy," Jessie said with another nervous glance at Simon and Stacy.

"Do it," Roman commanded.

"God, you're so bad," Jessie sighed. Then, looking into Roman's face, she slipped her right foot out of her Christian Louboutin *So Kate* high heel. Then she extended her leg so her stockinged foot was in Roman's lap. The tent in his pants was immediately evident.

"You feel it?" Roman asked with a grin.

"Yeah it's kind of hard to miss," Jessie said with a laugh.

"You want this inside you?"

"You know I do," Jessie said softly as she glided the sole of her foot over his erection.

Then she added, "You know, we've been lucky. Our dates have missed my period."

"So?"

"So do you like intercourse when a girl has her period?"

"Ugh. No," Roman said with obvious distaste. "But you've got your mouth."

"Oh my god," Jessie said with a laugh as she shook her head.

"So what does Ollie do when you've got your period?" Roman asked.

"We both go without," Jessie said. "He knows it's only fair, if I don't get any, he doesn't get any."

Roman laughed. "That's not how it works," he said.

"So how does it work then?"

"I told you. You've got your mouth," Roman said.

"What about me?" Jessie asked.

Roman shrugged and said "You've got your finger."

Jessie frowned at him. "Really?"

"I'm not Ollie," Roman said.

"I can see that," Jessie said, the frown still on her face.

"Look, this is how I am," Roman said. "If you don't like it, you can go home and fuck Ollie tonight. Who do you want? Me or him?"

Jessie looked down as she softly said, "You."

Roman grinned at her. "You know, I get you Jessie," he said knowingly. "You act like men and woman should be equal, and hey, I believe that too. But when it comes to sex, you don't want that. You want to be dominated and told what to do. So that means, when you've got your period, you blow me with your mouth, and you don't get any until after your period's over. Got it?"

"Yes, okay," Jessie said tersely.

"No, don't say it that way," Roman said chidingly. "Tell me if that's what you want."

Jessie softly said, "Yes, that's what I want."

"And why do you want that?" Roman asked.

Jessie knew what he wanted her to say. And she knew it was true too. She said, "Because I'm your little submissive slut."

CHAPTER 4

"I need to talk to Ollie," Jessie told Roman when they got back to the apartment. "About Simon and Stacy."

She added, "Don't worry. Just talk."

Roman nodded, pleased he didn't have to remind her of the rules. When she was with him, she belonged to him. Ollie was reduced to friend-zoned platonic friend.

Jessie walked Ollie into the kitchen. "We ran into Simon and Stacy at Per Se," she told her husband. She was calmer now, not panicked like before, but still felt anxious about being outed to people they knew.

Ollie's eyes went wide. "What happened?" he asked.

"I told them I got a part in a musical and had to change my hair," Jessie said. "They believed that. Which is true anyways. But Simon knew who Roman was and didn't believe it when I said he was my agent, and we were celebrating. Especially since you weren't there." She motioned to herself in the skimpy black dress and said "Especially since I'm wearing this."

Ollie slowly nodded as he took in the situation. "Even if they believe he's your agent, they might still believe you're having an affair with him," he said.

"What are we going to do?" Jessie asked.

Ollie considered a moment, then said "I'll talk to Simon tomorrow."

"What will you say?"

"I'll just repeat what you said," Ollie said.

"What if rumors start at your work?" Jessie asked. "Won't that hurt you?"

"As long as no one knows for sure, it'll be okay," Ollie said.

"So you don't mind if Simon suspects something?"

"I'll talk to him. It'll be okay," Ollie said.

Jessie studied her husband. She knew that rumors at his work that she was having an affair would probably excite him, the way the rumors at church excited him.

"I better get back to Romes," she said. With a helpless smile she added, "I'm so horny right now, I'm dying. I need fucked."

"What happened?"

"I'll tell you later," Jessie said. Then hesitantly she asked, "Would it be horrible if Romes didn't wear a condom tonight? I'm positive this is the safe time of the month for me."

Ollie was suddenly breathing hard. "To pay him back, for helping you get the part?" he asked.

"Yes, that. And you know, this is a special night for him," Jessie said as she touched her short dark hair.

Ollie stared at his wife. It wasn't enough that she cut and dyed her hair for Roman. Now she wanted to reward Roman by letting him inside her bareback. And this, just hours after she asked him to wear a condom.

"How is that fair? To me?" he said bitterly.

"I know it's not fair," Jessie admitted. "But it's bound to be that way sometimes, when you add another person. Right? You're my husband, but he's my boyfriend. And this is his night. So I want to make him happy tonight."

"Do you still care about making me happy?" Ollie shot back.

"Of course I do Ollie," Jessie gently said. "But it can't be tonight. You know the rules."

"But the 24 hour rule doesn't apply to him?" Ollie shot back, the bitterness still in his voice.

"Ollie, baby, come on," she implored. They both knew it was Roman who had insisted that, for 24 hours before their dates, Ollie had to wear condoms because he didn't like creampies. Ollie never insisted that the 24 hour rule work both ways. Because they both knew, because of his cuckold fantasies, he liked the idea of Roman fucking her bare, and shooting his sperm into her. The risk of pregnancy also got Ollie hot.

Jessie added encouragingly, "But you can watch us tonight. I made sure of that. I knew you'd want to watch the first time."

"The first time?"

"You know," Jessie said. With a teasing grin, she motioned to her hair again, and said "With me looking like this. My blonde hair cut off and thinned, and dyed black. Like how Romes likes me to look. Kinda, page boy look."

"God Jessie ...," Ollie groaned. The things she said. Her words tore him apart, but they were so delicious too. She was getting better and better at pushing his buttons.

"Is he sleeping over?" Ollie asked.

"I think so."

"And you'll sleep with him?"

"Ollie ... yes," Jessie said with some exasperation. "Listen ... I should get back to Romes."

Ollie curtly nodded. Jessie gave him an encouraging smile, but didn't hug or kiss him. She wasn't allowed. On this night, he wasn't her husband or have any husband rights. He was reduced to a platonic friend. All his rights as a husband – to her body, her affections – they all belonged to Roman.

A moment later, Jessie had rejoined Roman. Ollie hesitated before going to watch them together, wanting a moment to compose himself. Then his phone pinged. He looked at the screen. It was a text from Simon: "Hey buddy – Saw Jessie with a man at Per Se. Thought you'd want to know."

Ollie stared at the text for long moments. This was the start of it. The rumors at his work that Jessie was having an affair with another man.

Simon was not his friend. At best they were collegial colleagues. At worst, they were rivals. Ollie had no doubt that Simon would gleefully spread rumors at work that Jessie was cheating on him.

Especially since Ollie had heard Simon say he wasn't entirely happy with Stacy. They had two children, and after the birth of their second about a year ago, Simon complained that Stacy wasn't doing enough to get back to her pre-pregnancy figure. Ollie had heard him say "Stacy isn't as fuckable as before." It was a shitty thing to say about your wife, but that summed up the kind of person Simon was.

Ollie moved hesitantly from the kitchen to the TV room. He was surprised to see Jessie and Roman still in the TV room. He was even more surprised to see Jessie on her back on the sofa, with her skirt pushed up to her waist and her legs open.

And Roman was between her firm thighs, eating her out. That was the most surprising. Ollie had seen Jessie doing oral on Roman, but not the other way around.

"Oh god, god, god," Jessie moaned as Roman lapped at her pussy. She was breathing hard and her fingers gripped the sofa cushions.

"I'm almost there, don't stop Romes, please don't stop," Jessie begged.

Roman paused for a moment and looked up at Jessie. He said, "Don't worry Jessie. I'm not stopping until you cum. I owe you."

"Oh god ...," Jessie said, her words a grateful moan. Now she knew she could relax and enjoy Roman's tongue without worry that he would stop before she climaxed.

Then, as Roman returned his tongue to Jessie's clit, he pushed two fingers into her pussy. "Fuck!" Jessie groaned at the sensations.

Roman found her g-spot. He rubbed it and Jessie practically screamed, "Oh fuck!"

Roman rubbed her g-spot and licked her clit, with Jessie moaning and writhing under his tongue.

Jessie didn't last much longer. Within moments she was arching her back and wailing as the orgasm hit her tight sexy body.

Roman moved to sit onto the sofa. He pulled Jessie into his arms, her back to his front, holding her as she panted hard. Ollie was still standing, looking at his wife with her skirt still up around her waist, her shapely stockinged legs completely exposed, breathing hard as she recovered from her orgasm. He looked at his wife in the arms of the man who had just given her that orgasm.

It was always the conflict. The sight made Ollie's heart ache, but also made his cock so hard in his pants it hurt.

Jessie turned her head to look at Roman. "That was really good," she said.

"You liked that?" Roman asked.

"I really did," Jessie said, smiling at him.

Then they were kissing. Roman's hands roamed over Jessie's front. Then he moved his hands to her back to unzip her dress. She moved slightly forward to help him without her lips leaving his.

Roman unzipped Jessie's dress and pushed it down her arms. Now the entire little black dress was gathered around her waist like a belt.

Jessie had gone braless so she was completely naked except for the dress/belt, g-string, thigh high stockings and shiny black *So Kate* high heels.

Jessie moaned as Roman caressed her perfect A cup breasts, sexy flat stomach and long shapely legs. She reached her arms overhead and wrapped them around his neck, so as to completely surrender her body to him.

Ollie stood watching. His heart pounding, his breathing coming in quick short pants. His cock was so incredibly hard. Yet he hurt inside. Jessie had not looked at him even once. It was like she'd forgotten he was there.

Jessie slid off the sofa onto her knees. She tugged the dress down her legs and tossed it aside. She urgently undid and pulled down Roman's pants, freeing his long thick cock. It was hard and heavy.

Jessie moved her hands to her hair, and then laughed.

"What?" Roman asked.

"I'm so used to having to pull my hair to the side before going down on you," Jessie said smiling. "Now with short hair I don't have to worry about that."

Jessie's words tore at Ollie's soul. And at that moment, she seemed to remember him. She looked behind her shoulder and saw him. She looked regretful as she looked into her husband's face.

Not wanting to appear weak, Ollie forced a smile and said, "It's okay."

Jessie gave him an appreciative smile. Then she turned back to Roman and took his cock into her mouth.

Roman loved looking at Jessie's new short, dark hair as she bobbed her head up and down. As a blonde, she was the most beautiful woman he had ever known. Now with her hair short and dark, she was even more sexy and alluring.

Roman didn't want to cum this way. He wanted to look into her pretty face. So he pulled Jessie's mouth off his cock and moved her onto her back on the sofa.

He got between her legs and paused to put on a condom. Then Jessie said, "You don't need that."

"Really?" Roman asked, surprised. He glanced at Ollie looking a bit smug, knowing he'd worn a condom earlier.

Roman pulled the g-string aside and pushed his bare cock into Jessie's pussy. She groaned at the penetration. She was getting more used to him, to his size. But still, whenever he first entered her, the immediate sensations of stretching and fullness always took her breath away.

Roman began slow, and then gradually began fucking Jessie harder and faster. He put Jessie's stockinged legs on his shoulders to enable him to penetrate her even deeper.

It took Jessie a while to cum as he'd just eaten her out. But she did cum, crying out and her toes curling in the So Kate heels as orgasmic pleasure flooded her body.

Moments later as he banged into her, Roman growled "I'm cumming!"

"Yeah, yeah, cum for me Romes!" Jessie said.

"Where do you want it?"

"I want it inside me!" Jessie cried. "Cum inside me!"

Roman grabbed Jessie's hips as he came, pounding her with short deep thrusts as he ejaculated inside her. Jessie arched her back and rolled her head as she felt his sperm hitting her walls. It felt amazing! "God, god, god ...." she moaned as the jack rabbiting of his cock against her clit and the sensations of his cum spraying her insides made her cum again.

Afterwards, Roman and Jessie held each other, breathing hard and looking into each other's faces. With their bodies still tingling and basking in the afterglow of mutual orgasms, they both felt incredibly close to each other.

In that moment of intimacy, Roman looked Jessie in the eyes and said, "I love you."

Ollie still stood across the room. His cock was hard and he wasn't touching himself. When he heard Roman profess his love for his wife, he almost came in his pants.

CHAPTER 5

The rehearsals were grueling, both mentally and physically. The show opened in two weeks, so the rehearsals were every day, from mid-morning to early evening.

In terms of talent, Jessie was about mid-pack among the dance troupe. But she was the prettiest and sexiest, and also incredibly bubbly and friendly, so she quickly became popular among the dancers and the rest of the cast. The director and choreographer also quickly took to Jessie, so they were patient and supportive through her struggles to learn the dance routines.

Ollie canceled his business trip for the first week of rehearsals as he wanted to support his wife. He knew his bosses wouldn't be happy with this. He had to be careful, as this was no time to get fired. Jessie had gone on a leave of absence from her job, and the dance gig paid little. If anything, Ollie needed to travel *more* and close *more* details, as he needed bigger bonuses to cover their bills and support his wife.

Ollie felt the aftershocks of Simon and Stacy running into Jessie and Roman at Per Se. Simon went out of his way to talk to Ollie the next day.

"You get my text?" Simon asked as he entered Ollie's office.

"Yes, thanks, but no need to worry," Ollie said. "Roman's Jessie's agent and she just got a part in a Broadway musical. They were out celebrating."

"Without you?" Simon asked looking skeptical.

"Jessie and I celebrated the night before," Ollie lied. "I had some work to catch up on."

Still looking skeptical, Simon said "I don't know, Ollie. They looked pretty comfortable together. Like they were a couple. Roman used to be in the NFL. With the Jets. Do you really trust him around your wife?"

Ollie felt himself stiffening in his pants. He found it arousing to talk about Jessie this way—like she was cheating on him with another man. And hearing Simon say she and Roman looked like a couple pushed his cuckold buttons.

"Look, it's nothing," Ollie said, trying to keep the excitement from his voice. "He's her agent. That's all it is."

Simon slowly nodded and stared at Ollie, like he was studying him. Then he said, "Jessie looks a lot different with short dark hair."

"She had to cut it for the part," Ollie said.

"Yeah, that's what she said," Simon said. "She looks good though. Really good. If you don't mind me saying, she looked smoking last night. The dress she wore, it was really something."

Ollie felt his hard cock twitch in his pants. "Thank you," Ollie said, not knowing what else to say. He tried his best to keep his growing excitement out of his voice.

"I think she must've lost her bra," Simon added with a chuckle, as he'd been able to clearly see her nipples denting the dress.

"Look ...," Ollie began, as that comment was clearly out of bounds.

But Simon interrupted him, saying "She hasn't had children yet?"

"No," Ollie said.

"You're lucky," Simon said. "Stacy still hasn't recovered from our last one. Her body, I mean. I'm trying to get her to get a boob job. Perk them up, you know? But her pussy will never be the same." With a laugh, he added "Pregnancy is like getting your playpen bulldozed over. Enjoy Jessie while you can. With her face and body, I know I'd be boning her all the time if she was my wife."

Ollie felt his face flush as he thought about the prospect of Roman ruining Jessie's pussy. He said "Well, she's not your wife. So you'll just have to make do with Stacy's bulldozed pussy."

Ollie said this with a grin, and Simon knew he had asked for it. So as he left Ollie's office, he laughed and said "fuck you."

———◆———

Jessie was still in her dancewear when Ollie picked her up from the Duke Theater. Even though clearly exhausted, she still looked beautiful. He had to admit the short dark hair made her look more sophisticated and sexier. And with her sexy body in the skintight leotard and tights, the short hair made her body appear even tighter, and her long legs even longer.

They ordered carryout for dinner. Jessie was eating even healthier than normal, explaining all the dancers were weighted every morning and the director would go ballistic if a dancer gained even a single pound.

"That seems kind of chauvinistic," Ollie said.

Jessie shrugged and said "How you look is everything on stage."

They were sitting next to each other on the sofa. Jessie was still in her dancewear. Ollie ran his hands up and down one of her long shapely legs. "You look amazing," he said as he caressed her. "Your legs look so sexy in these tights."

Jessie gave him a weak smile. "Ollie baby, I'm really tired. I just want a shower and bed."

"Jessie, no, you need to give me a little time," Ollie said. "I've been thinking about you all day. And besides, I know you. You'll sleep better if you have an orgasm."

Ollie tugged the leotard off Jessie's shoulders and down her arms, exposing her braless breasts.

Then he slid down onto his knees on the floor. He pulled the leotard down her legs, with Jessie helping by raising her butt. Then Ollie curled his fingers into the waistband of the black tights and pulled them down her legs, tossing them onto the floor next to the leotard. She wasn't wearing anything under the tights.

Ollie spread Jessie's legs and got between her knees. "I need a shower," Jessie said, although she wasn't protesting too hard. Who would turn down oral sex?

"It's okay. I love your body like this," Ollie assured her. It was true. They often made love after Jessie worked out. He lowered his head and licked between her pussy lips. He loved her smell and taste. Sweaty, musky.

Then Ollie stopped a moment, and looked at his wife. God she was so sexy. Her perfect little breasts. Her flat taut stomach. Her firm thighs. Her shapely calves. Her slim pretty feet.

His gaze fell onto her neatly trimmed, sliver of a landing strip. It was still her natural color, blonde. He ran the flat of this thumb over the silky turf.

"Don't tease me Ollie," Jessie said. Her pussy lips had begun to glisten with moisture, anticipating the pleasure soon to come.

"Roman got you off with his tongue the last time," he said. It'd been a few days since then.

"Yes," Jessie said. "That was the first time he ever did that."

"He made you cum," Ollie said.

"Yeah."

"So he's good at that."

"He's okay," Jessie said with a shrug. "You're better."

"But he made you cum."

"Ollie, baby, if someone licks my clit, I'm gonna cum, it doesn't matter how good he is," Jessie said with a smile in her voice.

Ollie grinned at her.

"Now come on," she urged him, putting her hands behind his head and pulling his face towards her pussy. "You've got me needing this now."

Ollie worked his magic on Jessie's pussy and clit. He considered edging her, but he knew she was exhausted, and he wanted his turn. So after just a few minutes, Jessie rode Ollie's tongue to an orgasm.

Then Ollie quickly pulled down his pants and got on top of his wife. He had no intention of using a condom, or pulling out. To her credit, Jessie didn't ask either.

Ollie pushed in. He went balls deep without much resistance. "He's stretching you," Ollie groaned.

"Romes is ruining my pussy for your little dick," Jessie teased with a grin.

"Simon said pregnancy ruined Stacy's body. Especially her pussy," Ollie told her.

"Oh my god, what an ass," Jessie said.

"Roman said the same thing about Alisha," Ollie reminded her.

"No he didn't," Jessie said. "He just said Alisha's not as pretty as she was when she was younger."

Ollie didn't see a difference, and he hated when she defended him. But he decided not to pursue it as he didn't want to get into an argument.

"We haven't talked about the last time," Ollie said as he slowly moved in and out of his wife.

"Yeah ... the rehearsals have been all consuming," Jessie said.

"Roman said he loved you," Ollie said. "Has he said that before?"

"No."

"Have you said you love him?"

"No."

"Do you love him?" Ollie asked.

Jessie hesitated. Then she said, "There are all kinds of love. And different degrees of love."

Ollie's eyes got wide. "So you do love him?" he asked, shocked and concerned.

"Calm down baby," Jessie said soothingly. "When two people give each other so much physical pleasure, there's bound to be feelings. We've talked about this. You know I have feelings for Romes. And he has feelings for me. You know this. And you're encouraging it. Like how you want me to date him, not just have sex with him."

"So you do love him?" he asked again.

"Sometimes it feels like love," Jessie admitted. "Like when he's making me cum. Or right after. That's probably why he said that. It was right after he came."

"You didn't talk about it?"

"No," Jessie said. "Do you really me to talk about love with him?"

"No," Ollie admitted. "What would you say if he asked you if you love him?"

"I'd tell him the same thing I just told you," Jessie said.

"You'd tell him, sometimes you feel like you're in love with him?" Ollie said.

"No," Jessie said. "I'd say sometimes *I feel love* for him. There's a big difference Ollie."

Ollie continued to make slow love to Jessie. During this conversation about love, he had never grown soft. If anything, he had gotten harder.

"Sometimes I feel like you want me to fall in love with Romes," Jessie said.

"No I don't," Ollie said.

"Is that true?"

Ollie was about to answer no again. Then, after a moment's hesitation, he said "It scares me. It excites me too."

"Me falling in love with Romes excites you?"

Ollie shrugged. "I can't help it," he said with a helpless smile. "I know it's fucked up."

"So the other night, you were hoping I'd tell Romes I loved him?" she asked.

Ollie didn't answer immediately. His lust was rising as he continued to slowly move in and out of Jessie. This conversation was incredibly arousing to him. The idea of his wife falling in love with another man made him dizzy and weak with delicious cuckold angst and lust, and left him on the brink of cumming.

Yet, Ollie knew they were headed into dangerous territory. He felt like he was walking a tight rope.

"I don't know what I wanted," Ollie said honestly. "What if I wanted you to take the next step?"

"What do you mean?"

"Going farther than just sometimes feeling love for him," Ollie said.

"Is that what you want?"

After a moment's hesitation, Ollie honestly said, "I don't know." The helpless smile was on his face again.

"I guess, the fact you changed your hair for Roman, that's taken it to another level for me. It's like, you picked him over me."

"I didn't do it for him," Jessie said.

"But you're happy you've made him happy," Ollie said. He knew Jessie better than anyone. "I think you would have done it if he asked. You've done everything else he's wanted. Like the rings. You want to hold onto him. You want him to stay exclusive to you."

Jessie didn't try to deny it. Instead she said "I'd have to open myself up to the idea."

"What?" Ollie said, not understanding.

"What you asked me," Jessie said. "To take the next step. I'd have to open myself up to the idea. Like, lower my inhibitions."

"You mean, you've been holding back?" Ollie asked.

"Emotionally I have, yeah," Jessie answered.

"Would you like that? To stop holding back?"

"I don't know," Jessie said looking uncertain. "It's really dangerous Ollie."

"Risk is exciting," Ollie said.

Jessie stared at Ollie for a long moment. Then she shifted their bodies so now he was on his back and she was on top. "This is your favorite position right?" Jessie said. "You told me. Because you can get deepest inside me this way."

"Yes," Ollie said. "Missionary is good too, but this is my favorite."

"You know Romes isn't like that? Every position is good for him."

"Yes, I know."

"Does that excite you?"

"You know it does."

"Aren't you scared though?" Jessie said. "Romes is bigger. He's a better lover. If on top of that, I opened myself emotionally to him ... doesn't that scare you?"

"God Jessie ...," Ollie moaned excitedly. He was on the brink of cumming. "It does scare me. But the risk, it's thrilling too. I can't help it."

"You know how Romes is," Jessie warned. "If I give him more, he'll take more. And that might mean less for you."

"Oh fuck Jessie!" Ollie cried as he came.

CHAPTER 6

It was Roman's idea that he and Jessie take a break for the 2 weeks before opening night. This way she could focus on the rehearsal and get more rest and sleep.

Jessie understood the logic but she wasn't happy about going so long without sex. She had Ollie of course, and he had a wonderful tongue. But Roman was easily the better lover. And sometimes a girl just needed to get fucked really hard.

Jessie loved her husband of course, and she loved the intimacy when they made love. But after a week of no Roman, she was going out of her mind.

At about the 8 day mark, she and Ollie were in bed after another day of grueling rehearsals. They were making love, with Jessie on top.

She so needed an orgasm! Ollie could get her off with his tongue easily, but she craved a hard fucking, and she craved even more an orgasm from intercourse. In the past – before Roman – she sometimes would come from intercourse with Ollie. But now, after experiencing sex with Roman for so many months, her body needed a big cock to cum. Jessie wanted to feel stretched and full. She needed hot sweaty sex.

And Ollie, for all his other gifts, could not give her any of this.

The problem was solved the next day. The director told all the dancers that they should get a tan. Not roasted, but a little color. He suggested a couple of sessions in a tanning salon. He ended the rehearsal early so the girls could work on their tans.

Jessie headed straight for the tanning salon at Manhattan Motion. She hoped to god Roman was there. She wanted to kill two birds with one stone. She'd get a tan, and get her brains fucked out.

She sought out Brooke. "Can you check if the couples tanning bed is open?" Jessie whispered to her friend. "And tell Roman to meet me there?"

"Oh my god, you are a nasty girl!" Brooke said with a laugh. "Congrats on the gig, by the way."

"Thanks."

Brooke checked the monitor and said "Go to couples bed #2. I'll tell Roman to meet you there."

———◉———

Couples tanning bed #2 was a small room with a tanning bed large enough for two people. Once inside, Jessie peeled off her dancewear. She was sweaty from rehearsal and wasn't wearing any makeup. She hoped Roman still found her pretty and desirable.

Jessie needn't worry. As soon as Roman entered and locked the door, he pulled Jessie into his arms. "God I missed you!" he gushed as he kissed her.

"I missed you too!" Jessie said between kisses. She pressed her naked body against his. "My body missed your body!"

Jessie tore off Roman's clothes. "I need you inside me!" she said urgently.

"What about a condom?" Roman teased.

"Fuck condoms," Jessie said. She was too hot, she wanted Roman inside her bare, she wanted to feel skin-to-skin, she wanted to feel him cum inside her.

Once he was naked, Roman pushed Jessie to her knees. "Suck me off," he commanded. "Then I'll last longer."

"Romes …," Jessie whined, trying to stand back up. She wanted fucked! She didn't care if he came too fast! She'd just fuck him again! And anyways, she was so horny she'd probably cum as soon as he penetrated her, as soon as she felt those glorious sensations of being stretched and so full!

But Roman pushed her down again. "Suck me off, Jessie," he growled, his voice harsher now.

Jessie's cheeks flushed. She had missed this. Being dominated. Being Roman's little submissive slut.

Jessie surrendered, settling onto her knees. Roman's cock was hard. She opened her mouth wide and wrapped her hands around his thick shaft. She began sucking him off.

"Fuck you're getting so good at this," Roman moaned. "I'm not gonna fucking last long."

"Look up at me," he told her. Without interrupting the blowjob, Jessie tilted her face up to look at Roman with her sweet blue eyes.

"Fuck you're so beautiful," Roman gushed. "You know how much better you look with short dark hair? Tell me you'll keep it this way. Tell me."

Jessie took his cock from her mouth and said "I'll keep it this way."

"You promise? Even after the show's over?"

"I promise," Jessie said. "I'll keep my hair short and dark for you, as long as we're together. As long as I'm your only girl."

"Oh fuck yeah!" Roman moaned, clearly pleased with Jessie's promise. He pushed his cock into her mouth and put his hands behind her head. He began fucking Jessie's face.

Roman was hitting the back of Jessie's throat, and it took everything she had not to gag. Moments later Roman came, shooting jets of his jism into her mouth. Jessie's throat muscles worked overtime to swallow it all, and after he was finally done, she pulled away from his cock, gasping for air. "God Romes ...," she gasped.

Roman lifted Jessie onto the tanning bed, putting her on her back. He ran a fingertip between her glistening pussy lips. Jessie arched her back at his touch. "God I need to cum," she groaned.

"Ollie's not doing it for you?" he asked with a grin.

"He's fine," Jessie said.

"But you need more than fine, right?" Roman said, rubbing the flat of his thumb over her hard clit.

"Oh fuck," Jessie moaned, arching her back again. "Yeah, I need more than fine."

"You need my cock. Ollie's isn't enough. You need more than his little cock. Say it."

"I need your cock," Jessie repeated. "Ollie's little cock isn't enough. I need more. I need your cock."

"So who's pussy is this?" Roman asked as he pushed a finger into her.

"Oh god, shit," Jessie groaned.

"How's pussy?"

"It's yours, okay? It that what you want to hear?"

"Not good Jessie. You have to mean it. Or maybe I'll leave you like this," Roman warned.

"No, don't, please Romes," Jessie begged. "My pussy's yours. It's yours."

"That's better Jessie," Roman said. "But now you have to prove it."

"How? How?" Jessie asked desperately.

Roman rang his thumb along Jessie's blonde landing strip. "You have to shave this off," he told her.

"No, Romes, I told you, I can't," Jessie said.

"Does your pussy belong to me?"

"Yes," Jessie said weakly.

"Then shave it off," Roman ordered.

"But I told Ollie ...," Jessie pleaded.

Roman laughed derisively. "I think you know by now, I'm not Ollie." To illustrate his point, he pressed his cock head against Jessie's pussy lips. Hard enough for her to feel it, but not hard enough to penetrate her. He wasn't fully hard yet, but even in his semi-hard state, the mushroom shaped cockhead felt massive compared to Ollie's smaller manhood.

"God, fuck Romes," Jessie whined. She felt sexually frustrated, and defeated. Surrendering, she said, "Okay, fine, go ahead, shave it off."

"No Jessie, *you* have to do it," Roman said. From somewhere, he retrieved a razor and shave cream and placed it next to her on the tanning bed. Jessie realized he'd planned this.

"Please, you do it," she begged. "I can't do that to Ollie."

"You don't get an out here Jessie," Roman told her. "You have to shave it off. And when Ollie sees your bare cunt, you have to tell him you shaved it off for me. Because your pussy belongs to me."

Jessie stared at Roman for long moments, breathing hard.

"Do it Jessie," Roman commanded. "Shave it off. Prove your pussy belongs to me."

After another moment's hesitation, Jessie rose up slightly so she could see her pussy. She took the can of shave cream, squirted some onto her fingertips, then rubbed it onto her landing strip.

Then Jessie took the razer. She positioned the razer on her skin, between the landing strip and her clit. She hesitated, looking at the last blonde hair on her body. The last thing that proved she was a natural blonde.

Then she shaved off the landing strip. It was thin and already trimmed, so it only took a few swipes before it was gone.

Roman looked pleased, and triumphant. He pushed Jessie back onto her back. He climbed onto the tanning bed, getting on top of her between her opened legs. He used his hand to guide his cock to her pussy.

"You belong to me Jessie," he told her. He pushed his cock into her pussy. Jessie moaned at the sudden sensations of stretching and fullness.

"Not just your pussy. All of you," Roman said as he began fucking her. "But it's both ways. I belong to you too."

As Jessie stared up into Roman's handsome face, her breathing getting heavier as he fucked her closer and closer to an orgasm, he said "I love you Jessie."

Then Roman leaned down and kissed Jessie. She kissed him back. They were still kissing when she orgasmed on his cock.

———◉———

"Jessie?" Ollie called out when he entered their apartment.

"I'm in the bedroom baby," Jessie said.

Ollie found Jessie lying in the bed, wearing a robe. "You got off early?" he asked. He had planned to pick her up at the Duke theater after rehearsals, but she'd texted to meet at home.

"Yeah. The director wanted all the dancers to get some color. So I went to a tanning salon."

"Oh, okay," Ollie said, studying his wife. "You do look a little tanned."

"I went to Romes' tanning salon," Jessie said.

"Oh. I thought you weren't going to see each other until after the opening," Ollie said.

"I needed it Ollie," Jessie said.

"You needed him to fuck you?"

Jessie nodded.

Ollie processed this. Almost every night during this rehearsal period, they'd had sex. First oral, with Ollie going down on Jessie and getting her off. Then intercourse. But that hadn't been enough. He couldn't satisfy his wife. She needed more.

Ollie gulped, his throat suddenly dry. His cock got hard in his pants.

Reading his thoughts, Jessie asked "Does that excite you? That you aren't enough for me?"

Jessie's eyes moved down to her husband's crotch. She saw the dent in his pants and said "I guess it does."

"Where did you do it?"

"You know I told you they have couples tanning beds?"

"Oh yeah."

"Ollie, Romes knew I needed it," Jessie said. "He used that against me."

"What do you mean?"

Jessie opened the robe. She was naked underneath.

Ollie's eyes trailed down his wife's body. He got even harder in his pants, as her body was so tight and firm with little perfect tits and long shapely legs. He didn't see anything different, other than a little more color.

Then he focused his eyes on her pussy. That's when he saw it. Or, to be more exact, what he saw was missing.

"Your landing strip," he said, the angst churning his insides now.

"Yes. It's gone."

"I've asked you to shave it off before," Ollie said.

"Romes has too," Jessie said. "I told him I couldn't do it, because you've asked before, and I haven't done it for you. Today though, he said it was a test. To prove my pussy belongs to him."

"Jessie, really? You're my wife, not his," Ollie said. "You belong to me."

"What did we just talk about Ollie?" Jessie said, reminding him of their earlier conversation, about Ollie losing things if she opened herself up to Roman.

"So your pussy does belong to him?" Ollie asked bitterly.

Jessie ran her finger along Ollie's lips, saying "You can make me cum with your tongue. But not really with your cock anymore."

"Oh god Jessie," Ollie moaned, doubling over.

"Romes always makes me cum with his cock," she said, continuing. "I think that's why you can't make me cum, because he's so much better than you. Before you ask, yes, I can feel you when you're inside me. But you don't stretch me like he does, and you don't reach places he does. So since I'm getting used to all those sensations with him, and since I don't get them from you, it's hard for you to make me cum with your cock."

"Jessie, fuck ..." Ollie moaned. If she kept taking like this, he would cum in his pants!

Jessie sensed how close he was. She reached down and worked on his pants, quickly freeing his hard cock. With a grin, she asked "Do you mind seconds?"

She giggled as Ollie quickly moved between her legs and pushed inside her. Clearly, her husband didn't mind going second after Roman.

"Fuck you're so loose!" Ollie groaned. "He's wrecking your pussy!"

Jessie laughed. The way Ollie said things ... "wrecking her pussy" ... "ruining her pussy" ....

"It's his pussy to wreck, right baby?" she teased. "Romes' big cock gives my pussy so much pleasure. Shouldn't he own it?"

"You're fucking with my head, right?" Ollie asked as he slowly moved in and out.

"Maybe," she playfully teased. "Maybe it's a test for you."

"What do you mean?" Ollie asked as he continued to slowly fuck her. He didn't want to cum too fast, he wanted this to last.

"If you really want me to open my heart to Romes," Jessie said. "I told you, you might lose things. Maybe today, I picked Romes over you to see if you really want that."

"Jessie, fuck, god ...," Ollie moaned, burying his face into the crook of her neck. All this was so terrible. Yet, the hurt and angst were so deliciously arousing!

"Did he say he wanted you to shave it off so all your blonde hair would be gone?" Ollie asked excitedly.

"No. But he made me promise to keep my hair short and dark. I told him I would, as long as I'm with him, and I'm his only girl." Looking into Ollie's eyes, she said "So I picked him over you about my hair too."

Then she asked again, "Do you really want me to open my heart to him? You might lose more of me Ollie."

"But why does it have to be that way? Why can't you have feelings for him, but still be my wife?"

"I *will* still be your wife," Jessie said. "But I already have a hard time saying no to Romes. If I open my heart to him, he'll want more of me. And that might mean less for you. Or me choosing him over you."

"Like becoming a brunette for him. And shaving off your landing strip for him," Ollie said.

"Yes," Jessie said. She pulled his hands to her breasts. "And all that gets you hot, right?"

Ollie didn't deny it. "I'm close," he said with labored breathing.

"Go ahead and cum baby," Jessie urged him.

"I'm trying to make it last," Ollie said, his face strained as he moved slowly in and out of her pussy.

"I know how to make you cum," Jessie said as she reached behind Ollie and traced her fingertip down his crack towards his ultra-sensitive asshole.

"Oh god Jessie ...," Ollie moaned.

"Or maybe I'll make you pull out and not cum in me," Jessie teased. "I don't want to mix your sperm with Romes'."

"Jessie, god," Ollie moaned. "So you let him bare inside you? You let him cum inside you?"

"Of course I did," Jessie said. "You can tell, right? How wet I am? I don't want to make him wear condoms anymore. It feels so amazing skin-to-skin. And I love feeling him cum inside me."

"But you're not on birth control," Ollie reminded her.

"When I'm ovulating, I'll make him pull out," she promised.

"But that's not foolproof."

"You're the one who gets off on risk," Jessie reminded him.

"God Jessie," Ollie moaned, burying his face in the crook of her neck again.

He kissed her neck, and she immediately said "Don't leave a mark Ollie."

Ollie immediately snapped his head up. He bitterly said, "Why? You don't want any reminders of me on you the next time you fuck Roman?"

"Ollie, baby," Jessie said comfortingly as she affectionately stroked his cheek. "It's because of the show. I can't show up at rehearsal tomorrow with a hickey on my neck."

Ollie immediately calmed down. She was right of course.

"You're all over the place," she said.

"I know. I can't help it," he said, looking sheepish.

"I guess that's just how it is when you add another person," Jessie said with that same comforting voice. "Come on Ollie, cum in me. Be a man and cum inside your wife."

"You're saying I'm not a man like Roman?" Ollie spat out.

Jessie heard the anger in his voice but knew it was his angst talking. She gave him a teasing smile and playfully said, "You said that, not me."

Then Ollie came.

CHAPTER 7

The next day, the director ended rehearsal early again so the dancers could visit their tanning salons for a little more color. He reminded the girls to tan in the nude as some of the costumes were revealing (most were, actually) and he didn't want any tan lines.

Jessie considered going to Manhattan Motion but decided against it. The idea of seeing Roman again was tempting – *very tempting* – but sex with him was always so intense. Opening night was just a few days away, and she needed a relaxing evening with Ollie, and then an early bedtime.

Jessie took a taxi to a tanning salon close to their apartment. She was about to go inside when she heard someone say, "Is that you, Jessie?"

Jessie turned and her eyes went wide when she saw who it was. "Pastor John!" she said with surprise.

Pastor John studied Jessie's face. "Jessie, you cut and dyed your hair," he said. "I barely recognize you."

"I got a part in a Broadway musical, and I had to change my hair for the part," she explained.

"How wonderful," Pastor John said, smiling at her. "You look pretty with your hair that way."

Then the Pastor gave Jessie an up and down look. She realized what she was wearing wasn't appropriate for a conversation with her pastor from church. She still had her rehearsal dancewear on, black tights and a crop top. The tights showed all of her ass and legs, and the crop top went to just below her breasts, so her stomach was on display. On top of that, she wasn't wearing a bra under the crop top. For that matter, she wasn't wearing anything under the tights.

Pastor John's eyes seemed to linger on her braless breast in the tight crop top. Then he looked up into Jessie's face. With a smile he asked, "Do you have time for coffee? I've wanted to talk to you."

Jessie dreaded talking to Pastor John, as she knew there were rumors about her and Roman at church. But she couldn't say no. So she let Pastor John lead her to the Starbucks a few doors down from the tanning salon.

"I haven't seen you at service lately," Pastor John said after they sat down with their expresso drinks. Jessie also had a bottled water to hydrate after the rehearsal.

"Yeah, um, well, you know, I've been so busy with the new part," Jessie nervously sputtered. It was a lie of course, and she hated lying as she was so bad at it. In truth, she'd been avoiding church because of the rumors.

Pastor John gave her a friendly nod. If he thought she was lying, he didn't show it.

Jessie decided, if she had to have this conversation, she would ask something she'd always wondered about. She said, "I remember last year, I heard you tell someone you abstain from sex."

"That's right."

"But our religion doesn't require abstinence," Jessie said.

Smiling, Pastor John said, "You're asking why I abstain from sex, when it's not required. Is this a confessional?"

"No, um, ah ...," Jessie sputtered.

Pastor John laughed. He said, "I'm joking. I don't mind talking about it. When I was younger – my teens, early twenties – I guess you would say I was obsessed with sex. And it got me in trouble. And it hurt people. That's when I found God. And I decided to abstain from sex, like a recovering alcoholic abstains from alcohol."

"Oh," Jessie said. She looked at Pastor John – really looked at him – for the first time. He wasn't old, only in his mid to late 30s probably, and he was very handsome. And, since he wasn't wearing his robes, he looked to be fit. She could definitely see a young Pastor John as a player who was very popular with the girls.

"Actually, my prior experiences help me advise my flock. Like you and Ollie," Pastor John said.

"What do you mean?"

"I've heard rumors about you and Roman," Pastor John said. "And I've seen the two of you together."

Jessie's insides seized up. She sputtered, "We're friends, that's all. Since he broke up with Alisha, I help sometimes with his kids."

Pastor John gave Jessie a knowing smile and joked, "I thought we were in confessional."

Jessie looked away and sputtered, "It's just ...."

She didn't know what to do. How could she lie to Pastor John? It would be like lying to God.

"When I said I've seen you together, I didn't mean at church," Pastor John said.

Jessie stared at her pastor, fearing what he was about to say was going to be bad.

"I saw you with Roman at *Hamilton*," Pastor John revealed. "And I saw you again with Roman the other night at *Per Se*. You were alone with him. Ollie wasn't there."

Jessie was shocked. "What, how ..." she sputtered. "Why were you there?"

Pastor John gave her a friendly smile. "Even pastors go to the theater, and to restaurants sometimes. Although admittedly, it is difficult on a pastor's salary," he said. "But I will be candid, I was with lady friends both times, and they treated me."

"I thought you abstain from sex," Jessie said.

"I do," Pastor John said looking thoughtful. "But it's lonely without female companionship. I'm sure you understand that. To be completely candid, I've been reconsidering my commitment to abstinence. As you said, it's not required by the church."

"Oh," Jessie said.

They were silent for a moment. The Pastor's eyes again drifted to Jessie's braless breasts. She wondered if her nipples were denting the crop top, but she didn't dare look down.

"Can I tell you something?" Pastor John said. "Before I found God, I had a sexual relationship with an older woman. I found out she was married, and I told her we could no longer see each other. Even in my undisciplined youth, I knew it was a sin to be with a married woman. She told me, though, that she had her husband's permission to be with me. That he liked sharing her with other men. In fact, after she revealed this to me, he watched us together a few times."

Jessie's head was spinning and her heart pounding. "I don't know what you want me to say," she sputtered.

"I told you my prior experiences help me advise my flock," Pastor John said. "And you know what?"

"What?" Jessie whispered. Her cheeks were flushed now, and she was looking down at her hands, not able to look Pastor John in the eyes.

Then Pastor John dropped the bombshell, as he said, "You and Ollie remind me of that couple."

Jessie felt like she was going to faint. She felt like this was the worst moment of her life.

"I won't ask any questions," Pastor John said. "I am certainly in no position to judge you. I understand the temptations of the flesh."

Jessie was silent. She didn't know what to say.

"Jessie, I don't mean to upset you," Pastor John said with a friendly smile. "Please, compose yourself. Take a drink of your water."

Jessie quickly grabbed her bottle and gulped down some water.

"I'm actually offering to be your confidant," Pastor John said. "I was involved with that couple for almost a year. So I have some experience with such relationships. If you need someone to talk to, I am here."

"Okay," Jessie whispered. "Can I go now?"

"Of course you can go," Pastor John said with that friendly smile again. "You're not a prisoner Jessie. It's not like I have you handcuffed to your chair."

Jessie's head jerked up to look at the Pastor. He had a knowing look on his face, like he could see into her soul. Like he knew everything about her.

Jessie got up and quickly left the Starbucks. It was only when she was laying on the tanning bed that she realized that Pastor John's offer to be a confidant was to her only. He hadn't mentioned Ollie.

CHAPTER 8

Jessie was so nervous opening night, she was barely functional. She was certain she'd have 2 left feet and stumble all over the stage. But once the first act began, the butterflies disappeared and all the training and rehearsals took over. By the second act, she was having the time of her life, and it showed in her dancing.

The show ended with rousing applause and a standing ovation. There was great applause for the dancers, and although none of the dancers were singled out, it was still one of the greatest moments of Jessie's life. And for Ollie, he had never been prouder of his wife.

After the show, the cast quickly showered and changed. Then the cast, the director, the choreographer and the rest of the crew went to a nearly club to celebrate and wait for the reviews.

Hammer Malone, the producer of the show, also went to the cast party. Ollie was invited too, along with other spouses and significant others. Roman was there too. Ollie was anxious when he saw him, but was relieved when he was introduced as Hammer's friend rather than Jessie's boyfriend.

Ollie and Jessie's plan was to go to the cast party until the reviews came out. Then, they would go to a late dinner alone to celebrate. Ollie planned to get Jessie to bed as early as possible because for the foreseeable future, she'd be performing at least once every day, except Monday when most shows were dark. But before bedtime, he planned to make love to his wife, and he would make sure she came (although he knew he'd be using his tongue to get her off).

Hammer and Roman were standing on the other side of the room. Hammer was looking at Jessie.

"Jessie's very nice eye candy," Hammer said admiringly. "Very fuckable."

"You know she's my girlfriend," Roman said sourly.

"Your girlfriend," Hammer scoffed with a laugh. "She's married, right? That's her husband."

"He's her husband only because she met him before me," Roman said.

"Oh, come on, Alisha used to be hot," Hammer said. "Big tits, long legs. Not the prettiest face, but still a great fuck."

Roman couldn't help grinning at the memory. They'd had a few threesomes with Hammer. But that was when Alisha was young, when she was ripe. Now? He frankly didn't care if she was giving it to black dudes. Especially since he had Jessie. Jessie was prettier and sexier than Alisha ever was, even on her best days.

Hammer was still looking at Jessie. He said, "Gorgeous face. Tight body. Nice ass. Incredible legs. I don't mind the flat chest, although I know you like them big."

Roman scoffed but was grinning.

"So you gonna let me fuck her?" Hammer asked.

"When?"

"The night is young," Hammer said, grinning to show off his sparkling white teeth. Roman laughed.

The two friends had shared many girls over the years. It was give and take. Roman knew if he shared Jessie now, Hammer would share his girls in the future. It had always been that way. And while Roman doubted Hammer's girls were as good looking as Jessie, new pussy was still new pussy. And new pussy was always fine pussy.

Also, Roman knew about Ollie's "romantic plans" for Jessie tonight. It would give him so much pleasure to wreck those plans. Especially if it involved Metro Ollie watching his sweet wife getting gang banged.

Roman didn't have anything against Ollie. The trouble was, Ollie was between him and what he wanted. Jessie.

"Okay, but you have to keep your mouth shut about girls," Roman warned Hammer. "Jessie thinks I only cheated on Alisha once."

"Seriously? You're a bigger male slut than me," Hammer said with a laugh.

Roman grinned. What Hammer said wasn't true. But it was close to true.

"I'm only fucking Jessie now," Roman said.

"Okay, now I know you're bullshitting me," Hammer said.

"I'm serious. I like this girl," Roman said.

"You really care about her, huh?" Hammer said. With a toothy grin, he said "That'll make it even sweeter when I'm sticking my dick into her."

"Fuck you," Roman scoffed with a laugh. Unlike Ollie, he didn't get off on comments like that. He wasn't a cuck. Rather, to him, he considered it a challenge to show Jessie he was a better lover than Hammer.

⟹ ◉ ⟸

Jessie was with Ollie, chatting with some friends from the cast as they waited for the reviews to come out. From time to time, she glanced over at Roman and Hammer at the other side of the room.

The two men were looking at her as they talked about something. She instinctively knew they were talking about her. It was like they were appraising her, the way a man might appraise a piece of meat in a butcher shoppe before buying it. That's how Jessie felt, like a piece of meat in a meat market. She felt butterflies in her stomach, and her pussy began to tingle.

Jessie tried not to look as Roman walked towards her.

"Hey, can I talk to you a minute?" Roman casually asked Jessie. He was playing the platonic friend in front of all these people.

Jessie walked with Roman a few feet over to a spot that was semi-private.

"Hammer wants us to go to his place on the Highline," Roman said to her.

"All the cast? Is his apartment big enough?" Jessie asked, looking around the room at her friends.

"Just us Jessie," Roman told her. "Ollie can tag along if he wants."

"Ollie and I are going to dinner alone," Jessie said.

"Do you really want to be with Ollie tonight?"

"Of course I do," Jessie insisted. "He's my husband. We're celebrating."

"I get you're celebrating," Roman said. "I see you're pumped after opening night. It's like how I got after winning a game. I always wanted to fuck a hot girl. And lucky for me, Alisha was still hot back then."

"You're such a gentleman," Jessie chastised, but she had a laugh in her voice.

Roman grinned at her. He said, "So you're pumped. You want to celebrate. I get that. You know the best way to celebrate? Get fucked by a hot guy. Cum all over his cock."

"I've got Ollie," Jessie said.

Roman laughed. "Look, Ollie's nice," he conceded. "But I said you want to get fucked by a *hot* guy. Not a *nice* guy. And I doubt you cum on his little dick."

"God you're so bad," Jessie said, again with a laugh in her voice. "So what exactly will happen in Hammer's apartment?"

"I think you know Jessie," Roman said.

"So you used to share Alisha with Hammer?"

Roman nodded yes. "And he used to share his girls with me," he said.

"Maybe I don't want to be with Hammer," Jessie said.

"Jessie, imagine me holding you down as Hammer's fucking you," Roman said. "Imagine Hammer fucking your face, and me ramming you from behind, and you have to take it, because we're holding you so tight you can't move. Don't even try to tell me that doesn't get you hot. I know you too well Jessie."

Jessie stared at Roman. She was beginning to breathe hard.

"I thought you didn't like seconds," she said somewhat weakly.

"It'll be worth it to show you I fuck better than Hammer," Roman said with a grin.

Jessie laughed. "Don't be so confident," she said. "Maybe I'll like him better than you."

Roman grinned confidently. "That won't happen. Not in a million years. Like I said, we've shared girls, and a guy can tell who gets them off the best. Also I'm bigger than Hammer. He's not tiny like Ollie but not as big as me. And I know you like when I stretch you and fill you up."

"God Romes," Jessie said, laughing and shaking her head. She suddenly remembered she was in public and had spent too much time with Roman. "I better get back to Ollie."

"So are you going?" Roman asked.

"I need to talk to Ollie," Jessie said.

"He can tag along if he wants, but he might not want to," Roman warned.

"Why?"

"You think he'll be able to handle it?" Roman said. "And Hammer's got a foul mouth when he's fucking." With a grin, he added, "He's not a gentleman like me."

———◉———

A moment later, Jessie was talking to Ollie. They'd moved to another semi-private spot in the bar.

"You know, people saw you talking to Roman," Ollie said. "They're going to think something is going on."

"And I know it'll get you hot if there are rumors I'm having an affair with Romes," Jessie said with a knowing smile. Ollie didn't deny it. "Anyways, professional dancing isn't like a normal job. A girl who's faithful to her husband, it's like, what's wrong with you?"

"So you're always going to be cheating on me?" Ollie asked with a frown.

"Ollie baby, come on, stop going back and forth," Jessie said. "I know how you're wired now. You *want me* to cheat on you."

Again, Ollie didn't deny it. After a moment, Jessie said, "Hammer wants us to go to his place on the Highline."

"You and me?" Ollie asked, confused.

Jessie gave him a playful "*duh*" look. "You, me and Romes," she said.

"Oh," Ollie said. They both knew sometimes he was slow on the uptake. He was extremely book smart, but not as well verse with the real world. He said, "But we're supposed to go to dinner. To celebrate tonight."

"We can do that another night," Jessie said.

"So you want to go?"

"I kind of do," Jessie said honestly.

Ollie was hurt. This was supposed to be a romantic night for them. This was her big night, the opening of her first Broadway musical. He was her husband, she should want to celebrate *with him*, just the two of them.

But Jessie wanted to celebrate with Roman. And Hammer too. Once again – and it was happening more frequently now – she was choosing another man (in this case, men) over him.

"Don't give me that pouty look," Jessie said with a knowing grin at him. "I know how your angst works. This all gets you hot."

"You're going to be with both of them?" Ollie asked.

"I told you how Romes used to have threesomes with Alicia. He just told me Hammer was the other man sometimes."

"I'm just kind of surprised you're so open to this," Ollie said.

"We talked about Roman sharing me with Hammer," Jessie reminded him.

"Yeah, but that was abstract. This is real."

Jessie didn't respond. She just looked at her husband.

"You want to do this?" Ollie asked.

Jessie shrugged and said, "Romes is my boyfriend, and he wants me to do this. If you wanted me to do this, I would. I mean, that's how I ended up with Romes."

"But it's not all Roman," Ollie said. "It sounds like you want to do this."

Jessie shrugged again. "It's crazy, right?" she said. "A few months ago, I couldn't imagine standing here and talking to you about being with another man, much less two men. But things have changed. I guess I've changed."

⎯⎯⎯◉⎯⎯⎯

They waited until the reviews came out. When they did, everyone cheered. The reviews weren't earth shattering, but they were positive. Which meant the show wasn't one and done, it would continue on. And that meant, everyone still had jobs.

Soon after, the foursome took two taxis to Hammer's 6th floor apartment at the HL23. Ollie and Jessie in one, Roman and Hammer in another.

They were barely inside the apartment when Hammer moved close to Jessie and boldly put his hand on her breast, cupping her. "When I talked to your agent, he said you always rejected come ons," he said as he squeezed her breast through her dress. "He said that's why you never got any parts."

"That's right," Jessie said, glancing at Ollie who stood next to her. He was looking at Hammer's big hand on her breast.

"You're an okay dancer but there are lots of okay dancers," Hammer said as he continued to fondle her breast. "What sets you apart are your looks. You're good looking enough to get a steady stream of gigs. But you're gonna have to give it up."

Jessie's cheeks flushed. "I can't get gigs on my talent?" she asked.

Hammer laughed and said, "Jessie, honey, I thought I just explained that. Your looks *are* your talent."

Jessie's cheeks got even redder. She had never felt so humiliated. So objectified.

"Now just wait a minute!" Ollie said angrily, coming to his wife's defense.

Hammer motioned to the door. "You can leave anytime you want," he said. His hand still cupped Jessie's breast.

"It's okay Ollie," Jessie said.

"Yeah Ollie, it's okay," Hammer said, mimicking Jessie's voice. He laughed as he looked over his shoulder at Roman. Roman was grinning.

Looking back at Ollie, Hammer said, "By the way, feel free to take out your dick and jerk off whenever you want. Roman tells me you like seeing your pretty wife with real men. But use tissues, okay? I don't want your spunk on my floor."

Roman laughed. Now Ollie's cheeks were red with humiliation. But he made no move to pull Jessie away from the ex-quarterback.

"Now that we've got that marital misunderstanding cleared up," Hammer said with a chuckle. He reached behind Jessie and pulled down the zipper of her little black dress. Then he pulled the dress off her shoulders and down her arms.

With her eyes on Jessie's tits, he said "Take off your bra."

Jessie glanced at Ollie again. Then she reached back and unclasped her bra. She hesitated, then pulled it down her arms. She dropped the lacy bra to the floor.

"Very nice," Hammer said with his eyes on Jessie's bare breasts. "Small though. You thinking about getting a tit job?"

"No," Jessie said.

"You should," Hammer said. He reached out with his hands and cupped both her breasts. "Aren't you embarrassed to be so flat chested?"

Jessie's cheeks went red but didn't respond.

"You said you liked tiny tits," Roman reminded his friend.

"Yeah, I don't mind flat chested girls," Hammer said. "As long as she has a pretty face, and you have a very pretty face Jessie. I'm just saying, you'll never get a big part on Broadway with tits as small as yours."

Jessie flushed, feeling even more demeaned and humiliated.

"Okay, whatever," Hammer said. He put his hands on Jessie's shoulders and pushed her down onto her knees. "Go ahead Jessie. You know what to do. I've been looking at your sexy lips for two weeks. Now I want to feel my cock in your mouth."

On her knees, Jessie was eye level with Hammer's crotch. He was hard and denting his pants.

Part of her couldn't believe she was in this position. Just hours ago, she'd been performing in her first Broadway musical. Up until now, her impression of Hammer had been a reasonable, conscientious businessman who didn't mingle that much with the cast. When he did, he seemed affable enough, and harmless. He hadn't hit on her, and she hadn't seen him hit on any of the other dancers.

This Hammer was a different person. This Hammer was a creep. A bully. A thug.

But then, Roman *had* warned her that Hammer was a different person when it came to sex.

Jessie worked on his belt and then his zipper. She took out his cock. She saw that, unlike Roman, he was completely shaved with no pubic hair. His cock was good sized but not as big as Roman. A couple inches shorter, and not as thick.

But as Roman said, Hammer was noticeably bigger than Ollie.

She took Hammer's cock in her hands. As she did, she looked over at Ollie. He was intently looking at Hammer's cock in her hands.

Then Jessie opened her mouth and took Hammer's cock into her mouth.

Hammer groaned and rolled his head back as Jessie went down on him. He glanced over at Ollie and said, "Can't say I've ever had my dick in a girl's mouth with her husband standing right there. But let me say, your wife has a very sweet mouth."

Jessie worked Hammer. He was easier than Roman, since he wasn't as big. Hammer felt an orgasm building inside him.

But he didn't want to cum in Jessie's mouth. He picked her up and carried her to his bedroom. The blinds were wide open and they could see the crowded Highline below, but now Ollie and Jessie knew the windows were filtered so people outside could not see in.

Hammer threw Jessie onto the bed. The skirt of her black dress flared up exposing her long, slim legs. She was wearing thigh high stockings and black stiletto heels. Because she'd planned to be with Ollie tonight, she was wearing a thong, not one of Roman's g-strings.

"Fuck you've got great legs," Hammer growled as he got between her open thighs and ran his hands up her silky, stockinged legs. When he reached the thong, he ripped it off with a single tug, making Jessie yelped.

"You're fucking gorgeous," Hammer said as he leaned down and kissed Jessie. She kissed him back, opening her lips so he could push his tongue into her mouth.

They were panting when Hammer rose up. He took hold of his cock and pressed it against Jessie pussy lips. "Condom," she said.

Hammer shook his head. "I don't use condoms," he said.

Ollie found his voice. He said, "She's not on birth control."

Hammer gave both him and Jessie a surprised look. "Then this is my lucky day," he said with a laugh. Then he pushed his bare, hard cock into Jessie's pussy.

"You have to pull out," Ollie said as Hammer began fucking her. "You can't cum in her."

"You're standing in my apartment. My cock's in your wife. Do you really think you can tell me what to do?" Hammer derided as he fucked Jessie hard.

Ollie began to panic. He didn't think Jessie was ovulating, but he didn't want Hammer's seed inside her. But what could he do? Both Hammer and Roman were bigger than him. He'd have no chance in a fight.

But as Hammer got close to cumming, Roman took over. "Pull out Hammer," he told him.

"Fuck you Roman," Hammer said with a strained face. "I'm about to cum in this bitch."

"You can cum in her mouth," Roman said. "Now pulled out."

Hammer glared at Roman, but he pulled out. Roman flipped Jessie onto her hands and knees. Hammer quickly moved to her face as Roman got behind her. The two men penetrated Jessie at the same time, Hammer in her mouth, and Roman in her pussy.

As both men got close to cumming, Roman turned to look at Ollie. He said "Don't worry Ollie. If anyone gets Jessie pregnant tonight, it'll be me."

Then Roman exploded in Jessie's pussy as Hammer shot off in her mouth.

⟹ ◉ ⟸

Hours later, Ollie and Jessie were at home, in their bed. Jessie lay next to Ollie, naked. She was in a stupor, barely responsive.

She felt like that time in Roman's office, when he had role played "raped" her. That had been a life-changing experience for her, even though she had known he would have stopped if she told him to.

Tonight, she'd been with two men. Getting gang banged. Hands all over her, touching her everywhere. A big hard cock in her pussy almost constantly for hours (either Roman's or Hammer's, taking turns using her). Her face and mouth abused. Being helpless to do anything about it as two big strong men manhandled her.

It had been another life-changing experience. She was still processing it. Trying to get her head around it.

"How do you feel?" Ollie asked.

Jessie was slow to respond. Finally, she softly said, "Tired."

Ollie thought "used" was a more accurate word. Or "abused." "Wrecked." "Ruined."

He felt dizzy as these words flittered through his head.

"Did you like it?" Ollie asked.

"I don't know," Jessie said.

"You seemed to like it when they forced you," Ollie said.

At one point, Roman pinned Jessie's arms over her head as Hammer violently rammed her pussy, squeezing and twisting her nipples so savagely she cried out in pain. Another time, Jessie was impaled on Roman's cock reverse cowgirl; he held her head tight so she couldn't move while Hammer viciously fucked her mouth. Both times, her tight sexy body exploded with massive orgasms.

"Ollie, I can't talk about it right now," she said, impatience creeping into her voice. She was exhausted and barely functional, like she was in shock.

"They made you cum a lot," he pressed.

"Ollie, stop, I told you I can't talk about this right now," Jessie snapped irritably. "I know you want to talk to get off, but I can't deal right now."

Jessie's sudden rebuke was like a slap to his face. She hurt his feelings, and he felt bitter and jealous because he'd just watched her give all of herself to Roman and Hammer for hours, and yet now she wouldn't even talk to him for a few minutes. And yes he wanted to get off – *he wanted his turn*—but mostly he was just worried about her.

At that moment, Ollie felt like there was a wall between them, and it made him angry and anxious.

They were silent for long moments. Finally, Jessie said, "You know there's no show Mondays?"

"Yes," Ollie said.

"Romes thought it would be a good idea to go out Sunday night, after the show," she said. "I'll sleep over with him, and then, you know, if it got intense, I'd have all Monday to rest."

"So Roman just decided that," Ollie said bitterly.

"No Ollie," Jessie said, clearly trying to be patient. "He just suggested it. I'm asking what you think."

Ollie stewed for a few moments in silence. She wasn't giving him anything. Yet here she was already setting up her next date with Roman, after already being with him for hours.

"You know I fly out Monday mornings," Ollie said. "So if you're with him Sunday nights, we won't see each other for days."

"Ollie, I told you this would happen," she reminded him.

"So you love him them?" he spat out.

"No," Jessie said. "I mean, I don't know. I'm just trying to keep you and Romes happy."

"You're trying more with him than me," Ollie said angrily.

"And I told you that might happen too," Jessie said in a low voice.

"So you're always picking him over me now?" Ollie asked bitterly.

"Ollie, come on," Jessie implored. "Isn't this what you want?"

Ollie was silent. He couldn't deny it. Yet, he gritted his teeth, and it felt like his insides were tearing apart.

"Aren't you worried about getting pregnant?" Ollie asked.

"Romes didn't let Hammer cum inside me," Jessie reminded him.

"I'm talking about Roman getting you pregnant!" Ollie practically screamed.

"We talked about this!" Jessie said with exasperation. "You said the risk turned you on!"

"But you're not even trying!" Ollie said. "It's like, you want Roman to get you pregnant! You want his baby!"

Jessie was silent, as if counting to 10 to let things calm down. Then in a reasonable voice, she said "Ollie, you know that's crazy, right? If I get pregnant, I'd have to quit the show. After finally getting on a Broadway show, do you really think I want to get pregnant?"

Ollie was silent again. He couldn't fault her logic. But he was still angry. And hurt. And jealous.

"I'll be more careful," Jessie promised.

"Yeah, you'll probably make *me* wear condoms so *I* don't get you pregnant," Ollie said sarcastically.

"I – never – said – that," Jessie said slowly. "Ollie, the only times I make you wear condoms is right before I see Romes. It's his rule, not mine, you know that."

Roman's rule, Ollie thought angrily. *He's got me wrapped in a condom while he goes bare back inside my wife and shoots his seed into her.*

"Come here, baby, it's your turn," Jessie said soothingly, opening her legs and reaching for Ollie to get on top of her.

"I don't want a pity fuck!" Ollie said, his voice laced with hurt and anger.

Jessie looked shocked. "Why would you say that?" she asked. Rather than him on top, Jessie got on top of Ollie. She guided his cock into her pussy. "I don't want you to ever think that," she said, kissing him as she moved up and down on his hard cock. "Don't ever say that again, because it's not true." She kissed him again. "I love you Ollie. I love you."

CHAPTER 9

Sunday night couldn't come quick enough for Jessie. She wanted to talk to Roman about the other night with Hammer. It was like when you did something amazing with someone for the first time, like skydiving out of an airplane, or snorkeling deep into the ocean to explore a sunken ship. It was natural to want to talk about it. And it was natural to want to talk about it with the person who experienced it with you.

That's why it was hard for her to talk to Ollie about it. Yes, he'd been there, but he only watched, he wasn't a participant. And she couldn't talk to Hammer about it. She didn't know him well enough, and after that night, she was frankly intimidated and even scared of him.

Roman was different. They were in a relationship. Maybe boyfriend/girlfriend wasn't entirely accurate, but they were definitely in a romantic and sexual relationship. On top of that, he was her friend, a really good friend. So Roman was the person she wanted to talk to about the other night.

She had a lot of questions, thoughts and concerns to discuss with Roman. She had been with *two men.* How was she supposed to feel after that? Ollie couldn't help, he'd never done anything like that before. Roman had. Jessie wanted to draw on his experiences to help her process what she was feeling inside.

Maybe in today's world with porn so available on the internet, a girl getting banged by two men was nothing new. No big deal.

But for Jessie, it *had* been a big deal. It hadn't been just sex. Roman and Hammer had dominated her. Demeaned her. Used her body for their pleasure, with no consideration of hers.

She had gotten pleasure though. A lot of pleasure. She came so many times she lost count. And that was another reason she found it hard to talk to Ollie about it.

Ollie asked if she liked it. She said she didn't know. But she lied.

The truth was, she *had* liked it. The question that ran through Jessie's head was, *Did I like it too much?*

She wanted to do it again. That made her pause, as she tried to reconcile the girl she used to be, versus the girl she was now. And which version did she want to be? Did she like the girl she was becoming?

Sometimes, she felt out of control, like she was jumping off a cliff. It excited her, but scared her too. And it made her wonder who she would be after all this was over.

Only Roman could help her process these thoughts.

The musical continued to get good reviews, and the good reviews led to more people buying tickets. The shows weren't sellouts, but almost.

After Sunday evening's performance, Jessie quickly showered and changed into a clingy blouse, short miniskirt, stockings and high heels.

"You're looking fine Jessie," one of the dancers said to her. "You going out with Ollie?"

Jessie was about to spin a lie when Roman walked backstage. The guards let him in because they knew he was Hammer's friend.

As the dancers and cast watched, Roman walked up to Jessie. With a grin, he said "Hey babe."

Then Roman took Jessie into his arms and kissed her. Jessie immediately pulled back, and Roman didn't stop her. When she looked at him, he was grinning.

He did it on purpose! Jessie thought to herself. *He outed me on purpose!*

Jessie saw everyone was staring at her. She felt mortified! She sputtered a "see you Tuesday" goodbye and practically ran out of the theater. Roman followed her out.

"Why did you do that?!" Jessie hissed angrily after they'd walked a couple of blocks. Yes, the other night she'd told Ollie that professional dancing wasn't like normal jobs. Unconventional relationships were common. But rumors were one thing. Jessie didn't want her friends in the show to *know* she was having an affair.

Instead of answering, Roman pulled Jessie into his arms and kissed her. This time he didn't let her go when she tried to pull away. Finally, when he did let her go, they were both panting.

"I'm tired of sneaking around," Roman told her. "I want people to know we're together."

"We have to keep our relationship a secret Romes!" Jessie insisted.

Roman laughed, clearly happy. "At least you're not throwing the *I'm married to Ollie* bullshit at me," he said grinning. "At least you're admitting we're in a relationship. Maybe someday you'll say you love me. Since I've admitted I love you."

Jessie melted at his vulnerability. He was such a strong and dominating man, yet sometimes he revealed his tender insides.

"Romes, I'm just not ready to take that step," Jessie said gently, her anger gone. "I do have a lot of feelings for you. You know that."

"Yet," Roman said.

"What?" Jessie said, not understanding.

"You're not ready to take that step yet," Roman said. "Right? At least give me that."

Jessie's heart melted even more. "Okay. Yet," she said with a smile. "How about we say I'm *in like* with you. Okay?"

"Okay," Roman said, smiling back.

"But we have to be discreet," Jessie said gently, rubbing his muscular arm. She knew it didn't matter so much for her anymore, now that she was a professional dancer. But it was important for Ollie that her affair with Roman didn't get out.

They could deal with rumors. But if it went beyond rumors – if people found out the truth – then it would really hurt Ollie's career.

Especially if people found out it was more than a wife cheating behind her husband's back. If people at his work found out about his cuckold fantasies – that he wanted her to have sex with other men, and he got off watching her getting fucked by men with bigger dicks than his—then he'd be completely humiliated. Juicy gossip like that would spread like wildfire all over New York City and beyond, to other financial centers like Chicago, Boston and San Francisco. Ollie might have a hard time finding a decent job anywhere. His career would be ruined.

———◉———

They taxied to Roman's house and went directly to his bed. They were hot for each other.

"Hammer stretch you as much as me?" Roman growled as he penetrated her.

"No," Jessie groaned.

"He reach where I'm reaching?" he said as he pushed all the way inside.

"No," she whimpered.

"You like him better than me?"

"No," she whimpered again.

"He fuck you better than me?" he asked as he began fucking her harder.

"No," Jessie moaned.

"But you let him make you cum," Roman said accusingly.

"I couldn't help it," Jessie said.

"Next time, don't cum," he ordered.

"How can I do that?"

"You figure it out," Roman said dismissively. "When I share you, you only cum on my cock."

Jessie thought this was crazy. How could she stop herself from cumming if a good looking man who knew how to fuck (like Hammer) was doing her? But she was in no position to object as Roman's cock felt so good inside her.

"Okay, I'll only let you make me cum," she said as he continued to fuck her. He was doing that thing of hitting both her g-spot and clit, and she felt herself close to an orgasm.

"Do you cum on Ollie's cock?" Roman asked.

"I'm not gonna not cum with my husband," Jessie said.

"I'm not asking that," Roman said. "I'm just asking if you cum on his cock."

"No, I haven't in a while," she said. "Not since you and me started having sex. Do you like hearing that?"

"Actually I do," Roman said with a grin. Jessie laughed.

Roman changed his angle of penetration so he pressed harder against Jessie's clit. She moaned as his long thick cock slid over her clit for what seemed like seconds. And then, as his cock moved inside her, first the bulbous cockhead and then the thick shaft rubbed against her g-spot. The pleasure was so intense it was almost painful.

"So am I going to make you cum on my cock?" he asked.

"If you freaking keep doing that you will!" Jessie gasped. Roman laughed.

Moments later, Jessie came, screaming as extreme orgasmic pleasure flooded her tight body.

Then, as Roman got close, Jessie wrapped her arms and legs around him, preventing him from pulling out, even if he wanted to (which he didn't). She had told Ollie she'd be more careful, but at that moment she was so lustful and sexed up, she wanted to feel his cum splattering her walls. She wanted his sperm inside her.

As Roman came, he held Jessie tight as he said, "I love you, I love you, I love you."

At that moment, she felt love for Roman. She almost told him she loved him. But she held back. She'd done so much lately that hurt Ollie, she couldn't do that to him. She couldn't hurt him more.

CHAPTER 10

Roman had his arm around Jessie as she snuggled into his muscular chest. "Can we talk about the other night?" she asked.

"Sure."

"Are you going to share me again?" she asked.

"Probably."

"With Hammer?"

"Maybe."

Jessie got onto an elbow to look into his face. "With who then?" she asked.

Roman grinned. "I get you Jessie," he said. "You're submissive. You get off on someone else controlling you. Me. So you'll just have to wait and see."

"I'd like to know who'll be fucking me," she said dryly.

"You're not in control Jessie. I am," Roman said. "You're a little submissive slut, and you get no say on who sticks their dicks into you."

Jessie couldn't help shivering. Roman laughed.

"I'm kinda surprised …," Jessie began, but stopped.

"What? Tell me."

Jessie shrugged and said, "I'm kinda surprised you didn't both take me."

"You mean in your pussy and ass?" Roman asked. "I'm saving that one. I'm working on something special for you."

Jessie stared at Roman.

"Just remember. When I share you, you only cum on my dick," he said.

"I don't know how to do that," she said.

Roman reached out and took her nipple between his thumb and index finger. He squeezed and twisted her nipple hard.

"Owww!" she yelped. "That hurts! Stop it Romes!"

"Could you cum if I was doing this to you?" he said, squeezing and twisting harder.

"Nooooo. Stop Romes, it really hurts," Jessie said, her pretty face contorted in pain.

Roman let her nipple go. "That's what you do," he said calmly. "If you feel like you're about to cum, twist your nipples like that."

Jessie stared at him. He wanted her to inflict pain on herself?

"So did Alisha do that?" she asked, her voice strained at her nipple still throbbed with pain.

"No, I told you. Alisha was too much of a control freak. Usually she called the shots when we hooked up with other people."

Roman grinned and added "You're a lot more fun. I'm getting a better handle on how to use you."

"Use me?"

"You're a fuck toy, Jessie. My fuck toy," Roman said, grinning at her. "And it's a fucking blast playing with my fuck toy."

Jessie stared at Roman again. She shivered again.

"You should do what Hammer said," Roman told her. "I want you to put out for your next gig."

"You want me to humiliate myself for a job?" Jessie said sarcastically.

"I know you'll hate it," Roman said. "That's why you'll get off on it. You're probably getting wet just thinking about it. Are you?"

Jessie couldn't deny it. It was like being forced. She considered herself a strong woman. She was feminist, a believer in equality of the sexes, equal pay, right to choose. She found the idea of casting couches abhorrent.

But that was the old Jessie. She knew this new Jessie would bend over and let a man fuck her from behind, if that was what it took to get the next gig. If that was what Roman told her to do.

And she didn't know how she felt about that.

"Are you wet?" Roman asked again.

Jessie's pussy was tingling. Even though she'd cum just moments ago.

She nodded to Roman.

He grinned. "So this is what I want you to do," he said. "The next time you see Hammer, I want you to get on your knees, thank him for the gig, then suck him off?"

"You don't want to be there?" she said weakly.

Roman shook his head. "It's more fun this way," he said with a big grin.

Then with a laugh, he added "Then go home and give Ollie a big wet kiss."

Jessie stared at the wall behind Roman. Her cheeks were flushed and she was breathing hard. Her nipples were as hard as diamonds.

"Oh yeah, that reminds me, I got something," Roman said. He reached for a box. "I got something for Ollie," he said with a chuckle.

Jessie took the box. She hesitantly opened it.

Inside was a blonde wig.

"I want you to wear that when you're with him," Roman said. "So he can see how you used to look."

"You're being really horrible," Jessie said.

"I'm just dicking with him some," Roman said with a friendly grin. "You guys call this your game, right? So we're just fucking around, having fun."

Roman got on top of Jessie. He pressed his hard cock against her pussy lips. "You want this?" he asked.

"Yes," Jessie breathed, opening her legs wider and clutching the tops of his muscular arms to invite him inside her.

Roman pushed in and Jessie groaned. She loved the sensations of being stretched and so full.

"Whose pussy is this?" he asked as he fucked her.

"Yours," Jessie moaned.

"When Ollie's about to make you cum, I want you to pull the wig off," Roman told her as he stroked in and out. "So he'll see it's my pussy he's making cum."

"I can't do that to him," Jessie protested.

"But you will," Roman said. He leaned down and kissed her. Jessie kissed him back. Between kisses, he said "You will."

CHAPTER 11

Jessie stayed over with Roman. When they woke, Roman fucked her again. Around mid-morning, she showered and dressed to go home to her husband. As she was about to leave, Roman said "Don't forget what I said about the wig."

Ollie had delayed his business trip until Tuesday, so they could spend Monday together. His boss wasn't happy about it, and he worried he was close to getting fired. But he needed to see his wife before the trip, as he wouldn't get home until late Friday.

Jessie entered their apartment feeling anxious and worried. She clutched the box with the wig in her arms.

Ollie immediately went to her. He hugged her, then looked into her face. "You look tired," he said. "You should take a nap."

"I will," Jessie said. "But first I want to take care of you." She took his hand and led him into their bedroom.

They kissed, and Jessie felt Ollie's hard cock pressing into her upper thigh. She pulled away and said, "Wait, I've got a surprise for you. Actually, it's from Romes."

"What?" Ollie asked.

"I'll be right back," Jessie said, holding the box and going into the bathroom. She shut the door.

She looked in the mirror and saw a pretty, short haired brunette looking back at her. She barely recognized this girl.

Then she took the blonde wig out of the box. She studied it for a moment. The hair felt real. Maybe the hair was real. But the coloring was off. The blonde was too "perfect blonde," unlike her natural blonde hair that had light brownish streaks running through it.

The wig's blonde hair was fake blonde. Bottle blond.

Was this more of Roman "just fucking around, having fun"? But fun at Ollie's expense. Making Ollie see his wife with not just a blonde wig on, but a bottle blond wig. It was like another *fuck-you* to Ollie.

And she was going along with it? She was going to do this to her husband?

Jessie put on the wig. It was easy with short hair. Much easier than when she wore the brunette wig over her long blonde hair. The way her hair used to be.

She looked at herself in the mirror. Yes, now she was blonde again. The hair even went to the middle of her back, what Ollie called "bra strap length." But the blonde was clearly fake. It was like a joke, making fun of Ollie's preference for blonde hair. Was she really going to do this to him?

And why did her pussy tingle at the idea of doing this to her husband?

Jessie undressed, taking off all her clothes. Then she opened the door and rejoined Ollie in their bedroom.

Ollie's eyes immediately went wide. "What ...?" he said.

"You like me with long blonde hair again?" she said as she moved towards him. She stopped when she was an inch from his face. Then she moved her head back and forth, so the wig's hair brushed against his face. "Does it feel real?"

"This was Roman's idea?" Ollie said. "It's not even real blonde hair. I guess this is his joke, and I'm the butt of it."

Ollie had gotten it immediately. But then, he was very smart. Of course he got it immediately.

Jessie reached down and felt his cock over his pants. He was hard. "You don't seem to hate it," she said.

"You're naked," Ollie said, his voice laced with bitterness. "You were with Roman last night. He probably fucked you right before you came home, right? So of course I'm hard."

"Romes is just dicking with you baby," Jessie said with a kiss to his lips. She undressed him, and they got onto their bed.

"Like the other night with Hammer," Jessie said as lay on top of Ollie, pressing her naked body against his. "Roman said, if anyone was going to get me pregnant, it was gonna be him. I bet you almost came when he said that."

They kissed, then Jessie said, "I think he gets off dicking with you."

"I think you do too," Ollie said.

Jessie smiled and said "Maybe I do."

She reached between their bodies and cupped his erection in the palm of her hand. "You like it though. Right? You're so freaking hard baby. It gets you hot Romes turned me into a bottle blonde. Just like at some level, it gets you hot I cut and dyed my hair for him. You like it when I pick him over you."

When Ollie didn't answer, Jessie said "Just admit it baby."

Ollie hesitated, then said, "It just scares me. How much I like it. Sometimes I feel like I'm jumping off a cliff."

Jessie's eyes went wide as she stared at Ollie.

"What?" he asked.

"I said that exact same thing," she said. "I mean, to myself. I said it to myself."

"About what?"

Jessie hadn't gotten any answers from Roman. She wanted to see him last night to talk about the threesome with Hammer. She hoped he would help her process all her thoughts and emotions. But Roman didn't help her at all. If anything, he ramped up the intensity of the game.

She had thought Ollie wouldn't be able to help her, but after what he just said, she began thinking that maybe he could.

"You know the other day?" Jessie began. "You asked me if I liked the threesome with Hammer. I said I didn't know. But I was lying. I did like it. I *really* liked it. And that scares me."

"Why would that scare you?" Ollie asked.

Jessie was surprised at his question. "Because normal girls don't want to be gang banged," she said with exasperation. "You don't think that's weird? I mean, if you're at work, and a girl blurts out she loves gang bangs, wouldn't you think she was weird?

"You were with two men you find attractive," Ollie said in a calm and reasonable voice. "They both have great bodies, big cocks, and they know their way around a girl's body. On top of that, they both think you're super-hot, and that's got to be a big ego boost. I would think it's weird if *you didn't like it.*"

Jessie stared at Ollie. She'd been in major turmoil since the threesome with Hammer, wondering if there was something wrong with her. Ollie was starting to make her feel better about it all.

"What about this?" Jessie said motioning to the bottle blonde wig. "You don't think I'm bitchy for wearing it?"

"I'm not saying I like it," Ollie said. "But Roman's pushing things. I'm not gonna like everything he does. But you're clearly into him, and that's the whole point of doing this."

Jessie stared at her husband again. The way he normalized what they were doing – what *she* was doing – it was comforting. It was like, he was lifting a heavy burden from her shoulders, and easing her inner turmoil.

At that moment, Jessie realized she had been wrong to think Roman could help her work through these issues. Ollie was the one to help her. In fact, it had been that way their entire relationship. Whenever she was troubled about something, it was Ollie who made her feel better.

Jessie still had doubts. She worried about the person she was becoming. But talking to Ollie definitely made her feel better.

Grinning at him, she reached between their bodies and took hold of his cock. "It's time to take care of this little guy," she said as she guided him inside her.

"So I'm small?" he asked excitedly.

"I guess I always knew you were below average," Jessie said as she moved up and down his shaft. "But, I mean, it's a big difference compared to Romes. And Hammer."

Ollie stared up at Jessie as she rode his cock. He was breathing hard now. Jessie knew he loved it when she talked like this.

"You let him cum inside you?" Ollie asked, feeling her wetness. "You said you'd be careful."

Jessie took his hands and put them on her sexy flat stomach. "But you fantasize about Romes getting me pregnant, right?" she asked.

"Jessie ...," Ollie moaned.

"It kind of gets me hot too," Jessie admitted. "I guess that's why I like feeling him cum inside me. It's what Romes said, procreation of the species. You know, survival of the fittest. I guess since he fucks me so much better than you, I instinctively want him to get me pregnant."

"God Jessie, fuck ...," Ollie moaned. This talk was so thrilling! It was nasty and wrong, but he loved it!

Jessie moved her hand down and began playing with herself. "Don't cum baby. Not until I cum."

Lately, the only times Jessie could cum during intercourse with Ollie was by playing with herself. Knowing that, Ollie said, "Do you have to touch yourself to cum with Roman?"

"I've never had to," Jessie said with a shake of her pretty head. "Romes is way better than you, baby. He always makes me cum on his cock. I don't have to do anything."

"Jessie, god ...." Ollie moaned.

"Don't cum yet Ollie," Jessie said as she furiously fingered her clit. Closing her eyes, she said "I'm thinking about Romes. Is that okay baby? I'm pretending I'm with him instead of you, because that's the only way I can cum with your little dick inside me."

"Oh fuck!" Ollie moaned as he went over the edge and his body orgasmed. At the same time, with her hand rapidly rubbing her clit,

Jessie pulled off the wig so when she came, it was as Roman's short hair brunette girlfriend, not Ollie's bottle blonde wife.

CHAPTER 12

A few days later, Jessie got a text from Roman after the end of that evening's performance. The text said "Hammer is there."

Jessie had been about to go home. Remembering what Roman wanted her to do, she anxiously approached Hammer's office. She knocked on the door, hoping he wasn't there. But from the inside, he answered, "Come."

Jessie opened the door and stepped in. She quickly closed the door, hoping none of her friends had seen her go in.

Hammer was behind his desk, drinking something golden in a tumbler. Probably scotch. His eyes rose in surprise when he saw Jessie. "Hello pretty girl," he said with a toothy grin.

"Hi," Jessie said. She had butterflies in her stomach. After the other night, Hammer intimidated her, even scared her.

"Something to drink?" he asked. He didn't ask her to sit. This way, he was able to see more of her body.

Jessie nodded. She asked, "Do you have vodka?"

Hammer mixed a dry martini and handed it to Jessie. She took a long sip. She preferred her martinis dirty, but given what she was about to do, she welcomed the stronger version.

"The other night was fun," Hammer said. He was leering at her, undressing her with his eyes.

Jessie nodded but didn't say anything. She felt his eyes on her. She was even more uncomfortable now than when she had knocked on his door.

"You're a very pretty girl," Hammer said as looked her up and down. "Prettier than all the other dancers."

"Thank you," Jessie said with a small voice.

"Have you thought about what said?" Hammer asked. "Using your looks to get future gigs?

"That's why I'm here," she said with that small voice.

Hammer grinned. "Take off your clothes," he told her.

Just like that, Jessie thought to herself. *He knows I'll do what he wants. He's used to girls taking off their clothes for parts in his musicals.*

Jessie felt demeaned. She felt like a piece of meat. But she took off her clothes. In a moment, they lay in a bundle on the floor by her bare feet. She stood naked in front of Hammer.

Hammer looked her up and down. "Very nice," he said, appreciating Jessie's pretty face and sexy body. Her body was very firm, yet shapely in all the right places. Her long legs were amazing.

"You look like a teenager with that bare pussy," Hammer said, looking at her bare crotch. "How old are you anyway?"

"Twenty-five," Jessie answered.

"Still young," Hammer said. "But no children yet?"

Jessie shook her head no.

"So your body's still ripe," Hammer said. He twirled a finger, and Jessie turned around. "Very nice Jessie. You have a fine ass. Turn back around." Jessie did what he said.

"You're not on birth control?"

Jessie shook her head.

"But you let Roman cum inside you? You and your husband like to take risks, don't you?"

Jessie didn't answer.

"What's his name? Your husband?"

"Ollie."

"He likes to see you with other men?"

Jessie nodded.

"I saw him jerking off. He's got a small cock. Is that why you like fucking Roman?"

Jessie saw no reason to lie. With a whispered voice, she said "Yes."

"Don't you lose respect for him? He's got a small dick. He's jerking it watching you fuck a big cock. How can you have respect for him?"

"I respect him," Jessie said with that small voice.

Hammer shrugged and said, "No offense. Just curious. I've heard about cucks like your husband, but never met one."

Jessie looked down at her feet and didn't reply.

"Look up at me Jessie," Hammer said. "I like looking at your pretty face."

Jessie looked up at him.

Hammer looked at her small breasts. He said "Have you thought about what I said? Getting a tit job? Your body would be perfect then."

"Ollie is one of those men who likes small breasts," Jessie said.

"But if what he cared about mattered, you wouldn't be fucking Roman, right?" Hammer asked. "And I know Roman likes girls with big tits."

Jessie's cheeks got even redder, but she didn't say anything.

"Get a tit job," Hammer told her. "I'll even pay for it. With your face and legs, if you had big breasts, you might even get speaking parts."

Jessie hesitated. Then finally she said, "I'll think about it."

Hammer scoffed but didn't pursue it further. "Bend over. Put your elbows on my desk," he told her.

Jessie felt even more demeaned. *Take off your clothes. Answer all my personal questions. Bend over.* Is this really what it took to dance on Broadway?

Jessie did as he asked. Hammer moved behind her. Jessie heard him unbuckling his belt and pulling his zipper down.

He pressed against her back. Jessie could feel his hard cock pressing against her ass.

Hammer moved his lips close to her ear and said, "You know it's going to take more than this to get another job from me. You've got a pretty face and sweet pussy, but it'll take more than one fuck. You understand?"

"I understand," Jessie whispered.

"Now say, please fuck me," Hammer told her.

"Please fuck me Hammer," she said submissively, her cheeks going redder.

Hammer grinned. "I like when pretty girls beg," he said. Then he pushed his cock into her.

Jessie groaned when he penetrated her. Hammer wasn't as thick or long as Roman, but he was still big enough. He fucked her hard, each powerful thrust lifting Jessie onto her tip toes.

The situation she was in – being demeaned, using her body to get another gig, being under Hammer's control – it was like forced sex. And this got Jessie hot.

And Hammer's cock felt good inside her. The past few days, she'd only had Ollie to satisfy her body's cravings. And by now she knew that she needed more than what her husband could give her. Ollie knew that too.

Jessie felt an orgasm building inside her. She remembered Roman's admonition against cumming. So she moved her hands to her little breasts, and she squeezed her nipples hard. She squeezed and twisted her tender buds until she no longer felt like she was going to cum, but by then there were tears in her eyes from the pain.

"Fuck your pussy's so sweet!" Hammer groaned. "I'm gonna fucking cum!"

Jessie managed to wiggle free. As his cock fell from her pussy, she quickly whirled around and got onto her knees. She took hold of Hammer's shaft in both hands, rapidly stroking him. At the same time, she opened her lips wide and took his big cockhead into her mouth.

Seconds later, Hammer came and shot his load into Jessie's mouth. Her throat muscles worked overtime to swallow it all.

After it was over, Hammer leaned against his desk, panting. "I like a bitch who swallows," he said as he watched her hurriedly dress.

Jessie looked at him a moment more, then dashed from his office.

Ollie was there when she got home. "Are you okay?" he asked looking worried. "You're late."

Jessie walked up to Ollie. She put her arms around his neck and kissed him.

She kissed him hard with an open mouth. She pushed her tongue into his mouth, twirling her tongue over his.

She felt dizzy with lust knowing she was kissing her husband with the remnants of Hammer's sperm in her mouth. And her body was on fire after what she'd just done with Hammer. Especially since she denied herself an orgasm.

She needed to cum!

Jessie quickly pulled down her skinny jeans and panties. She pushed Ollie onto his back on their sofa. Then she straddled his head and pushed her pussy down onto his face. "Lick me Ollie," she urgently said. "Make me cum."

Afterwards, they were in bed. "What was all that about?" Ollie asked.

Jessie couldn't tell him. She couldn't tell him she'd just let Hammer fuck her to get another gig. She couldn't tell him she'd kissed him with the remnants of Hammer's sperm still in her mouth. She couldn't tell him she'd been extra horny since she'd denied herself an orgasm with Hammer, and that was why she had sat on Ollie's face and forced him to make her cum. She couldn't tell him she'd done all this because Roman told her to.

Maybe after all they'd done and talked about, Ollie wouldn't have been bothered by any of this. At least not too much.

But Jessie couldn't tell her husband, because she was ashamed. She wasn't sure if she liked the person she was becoming. In fact, at that moment, given the way she'd just treated her husband, she *knew* she didn't like herself. In fact, she hated herself.

"I know you need to cum," Jessie said. "You can fuck me if you want."

"That sounds like another pity fuck," Ollie said sourly. So many emotions were swirling through his head. Through his heart. And questions too. He didn't know how to voice them all.

"I'm sorry. I didn't mean it to sound that way. I'm just tired," Jessie said wearily. She was physically and emotionally spent.

Ollie sighed. There was so much to talk about. But so little time, with him traveling most weekdays, and Jessie having shows almost every night. Even on nights he was home, sometimes she slept over at Roman's.

But Ollie did need an orgasm. So he rolled on top of his wife and pushed his cock into her pussy. As was normal nowadays, he felt almost no resistance. He shivered at that realization. Roman was re-shaping his wife's pussy for his big cock.

Ollie slowly fucked his wife, breathing hard, his lust growing with each thrust. Jessie barely moved or reacted. Ollie knew she was getting nothing from this. Nowadays, she was getting all her sexual pleasure from other men. From Roman.

Ollie didn't last long. He never did nowadays. He cried out as he came, but again Jessie barely reacted. Instead, she affectionately patted his back and kissed his lips lightly. Afterwards, she rolled over and fell asleep.

CHAPTER 13

The show had been going on for about a month. Not great reviews or attendance, but enough to keep the show going. So the cast and dancers kept their jobs, for now.

Jessie sometimes wondered about what she'd do when this show ended. Go back to the job she hated? Or try to get another gig on Broadway? Especially since she was beginning to understand (and accept) what it took for a girl like her to get parts.

She, Ollie and Roman had developed a routine. Jessie was home with Ollie when he was home, except Sunday nights when she stayed over with Roman. When Ollie was traveling, Roman stayed over at their apartment. The "no more than 3 nights a week rule" was gone. No one ever talked about it, but that was the reality.

So, when Jessie wasn't with Ollie, she was with Roman. Sleeping and fucking in their marital bed. Ollie suspected Roman kept clothes and toiletries at their apartment, but Jessie was discreet enough to hide them so the fact she was spending so much time with Roman wasn't thrown in his face.

Jessie actually spent more nights with Roman than Ollie. But despite this, Roman was beginning to feel unsatisfied with this routine. Despite all he was getting, he wanted more.

Soon after he fucked Jessie from behind as she was bent over his desk, Hammer met for beers with Roman. "Your girl's got a sweet pussy, man," Hammer said. "Sweet mouth too."

"You know I sent her to you," Roman said irritably. "I don't want you to touch her unless I say so."

Hammer harrumphed and said "You're in a fucking shitty mood."

"I just don't see what Jessie sees in Ollie," Roman said sourly.

"You know what they say bro," Hammer said. "Opposites attract."

"He likes watching her getting fucked by other men," Roman said. "He jerks off to it. How can she respect him after that?"

"Yeah, I wonder about that too," Hammer said, remembering his conversation with Jessie. "So what are you gonna do? Break them up? Take her from him?"

"I don't know," Roman said with a shrug. "I don't want to be a complete dick."

"That's a first," Hammer said with a laugh. Roman grinned.

"You know she spends more time with me than him?" Roman said. "The idiot travels all the time. I mean, it's like he's inviting me to take her from him."

"It's not just sex. We like being together. We get along, you know? We've got a lot in common," Roman continued. "And sexually, I take her places Metro Ollie can't. I'm pushing her boundaries and she loves it." With a laugh, he added, "I think I've turned her into a nympho."

"You want my advice?" Hammer said. "Just keep doing what you're doing. If she keeps spending more time with you than him, pretty soon she'll be living with you, and he'll be out of the picture completely. And you won't be the bad guy. It'll just naturally happen."

Roman considered his friend's advice. With a nod, he said, "Yeah, that's what I'll do."

CHAPTER 14

It was Sunday after the evening's show. Jessie was at Roman's. As usual on Sundays, she was staying over with him.

They were in his bed, kissing. Roman was still dressed. Jessie was naked except for stockings and her favorite, shiny black *So Kate* high heels.

"Tonight's going to be intense," Roman warned between kisses.

"Oh yeah?" Jessie said as she kissed him back.

"You won't like it," he told her. He put his hand over her mound. "But this is my pussy. You don't decide who goes inside you. I decide."

Jessie shivered at Roman's words. At what was to come.

"Am I right?"

"Yes," Jessie breathed.

"Say it," he ordered.

"You own my pussy," Jessie said as she continued to kiss Roman. "You own my body."

"Not Ollie," Roman said.

"Not Ollie," Jessie agreed. "You decide who fucks me. Not Ollie. Not me. You do."

"That's right Jessie," Roman said. Then with a quick movement, he pulled Jessie's arms above her head and he handcuffed her to the bed posts.

"What?" Jessie asked, surprised. They'd never done this before.

Roman moved to Jessie's feet. He cuffed her ankles to the posts there. She was spreadeagled, unable to love.

"Romes, what?" Jessie asked again.

Roman moved to her pretty face. From somewhere, he produced a ball gag. He forced the gang into her mouth, and then ran the strap around her head. Now Jessie couldn't move and couldn't speak.

Jessie's eyes looked questioningly up at Roman. *What's going on?* she silently asked.

"I've shared you with a man. Hammer," Roman said as he lazily ran his fingertips over her bare breasts. "Tonight, I'm sharing you with a girl. Two girls actually."

Jessie's eyes opened wide with surprise.

And then the two girls walked into the room. Jessie screamed into the ball gag when she saw who they were.

It was Fletcher and Bianca!

They were both young and pretty, with short dark hair. Unlike Jessie's slim tight figure and smallish breasts, both girls had classic hourglass figures with big DD breasts.

The two girls actually looked like twins, or at least sisters. Especially since they were wearing the same thing. Black leather corsets, black stockings, and shiny high heeled boots. They looked like S&M dominatrices, especially since they both carried leather whips and paddles.

And big black dildos were attached to the crotches of their corsets!

"Hello Jessie," Fletcher said menacingly as both girls walked towards her. Jessie screamed into the ball gag again, and struggled against the restraints.

The girls stopped when they got to Roman. Fletcher gave him a big open mouth kiss, and then Bianca did the same. Bianca said, "Roman says your husband likes seeing him fucking you. Maybe you'll like seeing us fucking Roman." To emphasize her point, both girls lowered their hands and rubbed Roman's erection over his pants.

Jessie looked imploringly at Roman, frantically shaking her head. *She didn't want this! She didn't want this!*

Bianca and Fletcher got on the bed with Jessie, Bianca on her right and Fletcher on her left.

The girls immediately began caressing Jessie's body. "Oh Jessie baby, your body's so firm and tight," Bianca cooed as Fletcher grinned. Then Briana moved her hand to Jessie's bare crotch. "And look, you have no hair down here. Is that your thing, Jessie, the barely legal look?" The two girls laughed.

Fletcher ran her fingers through Jessie's short dark hair. "I see you changed your hair," she said. "Now you look just like us."

Then Bianca squeezed Jessie's tits hard, and said, "Except you're a flat chested bitch."

Both Bianca and Fletcher laughed again. Standing at the foot of the bed, Roman grinned.

"Remember, don't let her cum," Roman reminded them.

"Don't worry. Pretty Jessie's not getting any pleasure from us," Fletcher said. Then abruptly, the two girls flipped Jessie over so she was on her stomach. Jessie realized the handcuffs had some kind of swivel mechanism so they could rotate her while still keeping her spreadeagled.

"Look at this tight ass," Fletcher said as she caressed Jessie's shapely, firm cheeks. "I bet you're proud of your ass."

Then suddenly, Fletcher spanked Jessie's ass with the paddle. "A perfect ass like this is begging to be spanked," she said as she slapped Jessie's tender cheeks again. Jessie groaned in pain with each slap.

"Don't leave any marks," Roman said. "She's got a show tomorrow."

Fletcher leaned down and looked into Jessie's eyes. She was tearing up from the pain, and she looked scared. "I guess no more spanking," Fletcher said flippantly. "Don't worry. We brought another toy and it doesn't leave any marks."

Jessie looked even more scared as from somewhere, Fletcher produced a curling iron. It was plugged in and Jessie saw it was on the high setting.

"We've all used curling irons, right Jessie?" Fletcher said. "It hurts but not enough to burn skin. Have you ever felt it on your ass?"

"No, no, no!" Jessie cried into the ball gag, furiously shaking her head. Then she screamed as Fletcher pressed the point of the curling iron on one of her tender ass cheeks.

"Here, let me help," Bianca said, and Jessie felt the younger girl pull her ass cheeks apart.

"Noooooo!" Jessie screamed into the ball gag, and she cried out in pain again as Fletcher traced the point of the curling iron between her super sensitive ass cheeks.

"Enough," Roman said. Bianca and Fletcher laughed and handed the curling iron to him.

Then they flipped Jessie over so she was on her back again. Fletcher ran her fingers over Jessie's face, saying "You think you're so pretty. And I admit, you're prettier than me. But you won't be so pretty after we're done with you."

Jessie furiously shook her head and again tried to pull away, but the handcuffs held her tight. She tried to shrink into the pillow as both Fletcher and Bianca approached her face with magic markers. "These are permanent markers, Jessie," Bianca said.

"Yeah. We're about to tattoo your face," Fletcher said. "I don't think you're gonna look as pretty anymore Jessie."

Jessie cried "No, no, no!" into the ball gag but the two younger girls ignored her. She sobbed and tears rolled down her cheeks as they drew wide black marks all over her pretty face.

Then they held a mirror so Jessie could see herself. She sobbed even harder as she saw her face covered with thick lines of black permanent markers.

"Now it's time for the real fun," Bianca said. She got between Jessie's spread legs. She rubbed lube onto the thick black dildo between her legs. Then she penetrated Jessie with the dildo. Jessie groaned at the sudden penetration of her pussy.

The girls quickly shifted Jessie so she was on her side. Then from behind, Fletcher pushed her lubricated dildo into Jessie's ass. Jessie cried out in pain into the gag.

For the first time in her life, Jessie was double penetrated. But not by men. By two spiteful girls with big black strap-on dildos.

The girls began fucking Jessie's pussy and ass. They fucked her hard. She cried and whined but there was nothing she could do. She just had to take it, getting fucked up both her holes.

But then gradually, her body began to respond. Bianca and Fletcher were in sync with their thrusts. And, as they fucked her, the girls played with Jessie's nipples and clit. On top of that, the dildos were actually vibrators, so they reverberated inside Jessie and against her clit as the girls fucked her.

Jessie didn't want to cum. She didn't want to let these evil girls make her cum. Not after what they'd done to her.

But Jessie's body betrayed her. Soon she was moaning into the ball gag, her body writhing from the fucking she was getting from Bianca and Fletcher.

Then moments later, Jessie's back arched and she cried out into the ball gag – this time in pleasure – as a massive orgasm ripped through her sexy body.

Bianca and Fletcher laughed and high fived as they felt Jessie orgasm. Then suddenly, they pulled out of her. Just as suddenly, Jessie was released from the handcuffs, and the ball gag was removed from her mouth.

Before Jessie could move, Roman was between her legs and fucking her with his big cock. "You let them make you cum Jessie," he growled at her. "Now it's going to be even worse next time."

Roman fucked Jessie hard for a long time. She came over and over again. At one point she glanced over at Bianca and Fletcher. The two young girls were naked now and in the 69 position, eating each other.

Finally Roman roared and came, shooting his hot virile sperm into Jessie's unprotected, fertile pussy.

Roman rolled to the side and collapsed next to Jessie, panting hard.

Bianca and Fletcher were suddenly by her side. They were dressed and looking guilty. "Sorry if we hurt you," Bianca said. "Roman said you're into that."

Fletcher had some baby wipes in her hand. "We were just shitting you," she said as she gently wiped Jessie's face. "It's not permanent marker."

After she finished wiping Jessie's face, she moved the mirror so Jessie could see herself. All the black lines were gone.

"You've probably figured out, me and Fletcher like boys and girls," Bianca said. "And you're really pretty, and sexy. Maybe we can get together and play again."

Then both Bianca and Fletcher kissed Jessie on the lips, and moments later they were gone.

They left Jessie breathing hard and staring up at the ceiling, her head spinning and feeling stunned.

CHAPTER 15

"It was like being raped," Jessie said to Ollie later that week when he was back home. "I mean, not really, but sort of. More like the real thing than anything else Romes has done to me. I mean, I knew he would have stopped if I told him to, but still ...."

Ollie was staring off to the side, processing the story Jessie had just told him.

"But I guess I knew deep down Romes wouldn't really let them hurt me," Jessie continued. "So I guess, maybe, I liked it? I don't know. I'm still processing it."

"You said the girls made you cum," Ollie said.

Jessie nodded. She said, "And Ollie, god, I think it's the hardest I've ever cum in my life. I mean, it was more intense than even with Romes."

"So that's why you think you liked it?" Ollie asked.

Jessie nodded. "I mean, if I didn't like it, you know, like at a basic visceral human level, then I wouldn't have cum so hard, right?"

"But Jessie – they said they were going to tattoo your face," Ollie said.

"I know. I was so scared," Jessie admitted, and she shivered at the memory. "And the curling iron really hurt. I was afraid they'd use it on my nipples. Or even my clit. Or even push it into me." She shivered again.

"Did they touch your asshole with it?"

Jessie shook her head. "No, they didn't touch me there," she said. "So I guess maybe they knew what they were doing. You know, pain but not too much pain."

With a laugh, Jessie said "Maybe they use the curling iron on each other."

Ollie was silent for long moments. Finally, Jessie asked, "What are you thinking baby?"

"It's just …," Ollie sputtered. He was trying to come to grips with his thoughts and emotions.

Composing his thoughts, he said, "Each time Roman pushes your boundaries, I feel like he's pushing you away from me. Because you love what he does to you, and I can never do to you what he does. So it's like, he's driving a wedge between us."

"I'm worried about where all this is going too," Jessie said looking concerned. "I used to be this person, and now I'm a different person, and that scares me."

"Yeah, but you're loving it all, right?" Ollie said with resignation. "So I think you like the new you."

Jessie wasn't so sure. She was still ashamed about what she'd done the other day after being with Hammer. She'd kissed Ollie after Hammer had cum in her mouth. Then she sat on his face and forced him to lick her to orgasm. She'd been really mean to her husband, and to make it worse, she'd done the cum kiss because Roman told her too. Jessie still hadn't been able to bring herself to confess all this to Ollie.

Jessie and Ollie were silent for long moments. "Have you told him you love him?" he asked.

"No," Jessie answered.

"Do you love him?"

"You told me to open my heart to him," Jessie said defensively.

"I know I did," Ollie said. "I'm just asking—do you love him?"

"I don't know Ollie," Jessie said. "Maybe I do. Maybe. I don't know."

Then she said, "Sometimes I think you want me to fall in love with Romes. Do you?"

Ollie stared at his wife, his insides churning. Their game had turned very dangerous. He felt on the verge of losing his wife to Roman.

Yet, his cock was so incredibly hard. He said, "I don't know."

Then Ollie moved on top of Jessie, kissing her and running his hands over her body.

Ollie pulled her skirt up, then pulled her panties down her long, lovely legs. He pulled out his cock and got into position to mount her.

But Jessie stopped him with a hand to his chest. "You have to wear a condom, Ollie," she told him. "I might see Romes tomorrow."

"Is that fair?" Ollie said, his voice laced with bitterness. "I have to wear a condom with my wife because you *might* see him tomorrow?"

"I'm supposed to be his girlfriend," Jessie said. "I'm the only girl he has sex with. So ...."

"I know that Jessie," Ollie snapped irritably. "So when he's horny, you pick him over me. Is that fair? I just got home. Don't I ever come first?"

"I'm sorry Ollie. You're right," Jessie said, giving in completely. She pulled him towards her. "Come make love to me. You don't have to wear a condom."

Ollie was angry, hurt and jealous. Once again he felt like she was only fucking him out of pity. A pity fuck.

"Forget it," Ollie said, rolling off Jessie.

"Ollie, please," Jessie said reaching for him.

"Just forget it Jessie," Ollie said bitterly. "Do whatever you want to do tomorrow. See Roman. Fuck him. Spend the night with him. Whatever."

"I'm sorry, I'm wrong," Jessie said, apologizing. "You're completely right. I won't see Romes tomorrow. I'm come home right after the show."

"Fine, then, whatever," Ollie said. He was angry, frustrated, jealous, scared ....

He rolled over and said, "I've got to get to work early tomorrow anyway."

They were silent after that. It took both of them a long time to fall asleep.

CHAPTER 16

"Roman, right? Remember me?"

Roman looked at the man who had just walked into his gym. Then he remembered. "Simon, right? You work with Ollie. I ran into you and your wife at Per Se."

"Right. My wife's Stacy," Simon said.

"Yes, right," Roman said. "I remember. Stacy."

"And you were with Jessie," Simon said.

"That's right," Roman said.

Looking around, Simon said "Is there a place we can talk in private?"

<hr>

A few minutes later, they were in Roman's office. "So what's up?" Roman asked.

Simon put a folder on Roman's desk. "I set up investments for rich people," he said. "High return, low risk, with substantial buy ins."

"Why are you telling me this?" Roman asked. "I'm sure I don't have the money for the buy in."

"Not unless you're a billionaire," Simon said.

Roman scoffed. He was doing well for himself, but he was no Jeff Bezos.

"So why are you telling me this?" he asked again.

"I can get you in," Simon said. "Twenty, thirty thousand. That's all it'll take. And your money will double in six months. And then double again in a year. If you keep the money in, pretty soon you'll be a millionaire. And it'll keep growing."

Roman looked interested. He could pull together twenty thousand dollars. But also skeptical. "So why would you do that for me?" he asked.

"Jessie," Simon said.

"What about Jessie?" Roman said.

"I've heard rumors," Simon said. "I know people who go to the church Jessie and Ollie go to. They say you and Jessie are having an affair."

Roman didn't deny it. And he saw through Simon immediately.

"So let me get this straight," Roman said. "I help you get into Jessie's pants, and you get me into this investment."

"You got it," Simon said.

"And you'd fuck her, even though she's married to a guy you work with?" Roman asked.

"You think Ollie and I are friends?" Simon scoffed, shaking his head. On Wall Street, you didn't have friends. Everyone was a shark, out for themselves. And he resented Ollie because he had a super hot wife like Jessie, while he was stuck with Stacy whose best days were way in the past.

"It'll be even sweeter to fuck Jessie because I'll also be fucking over Ollie," Simon said.

Roman laughed, and said, "You know Simon, I like you."

The two men grinned at each other.

Roman said "I'm divorcing my bitch wife."

Simon understood. He said, "I can hide the money. She'll never get her greedy hands on it."

Roman's grin got bigger. He extended his hand. "Deal," he said, and the two men shook hands.

<hr>

It was Sunday night, and Jessie was at Roman's as usual.

She was in his bed, naked except for silky lingerie that left little to the imagination, and high heels.

Tonight, though, she wasn't tied up, and didn't have a gag in her mouth.

"I'm sharing you tonight," Roman said. "With another man."

"Okay," Jessie said, a shiver of excitement running down her spine and tinkling her pussy. "Who?"

Roman put an eye mask on Jessie so she couldn't see. "That's the point of tonight," he said. "You're not going to be able to see the man fucking you. Maybe it's a black man. An old man. A teenager. A street bum. You're not gonna know until after he's done with you."

The eye mask was secured tightly on Jessie. She couldn't see a thing.

"Don't try to take the mask off," Roman told her.

"I won't," Jessie promised.

"We'll call him DK, for Dark Knight," Roman said. He wanted Jessie to think Simon was a black man so she wouldn't know who he was. Until the end.

Roman looked to the door and said "Okay, DK. She's ready."

Simon walked into the room. He was naked. Roman had to admit that Simon had a good body. And his cock was big. Not as big as his, but bigger than Hammer's. And way bigger than Metro Ollie's.

Simon walked to the foot of the bed and looked at the young married girl laying there.

"Holy fuck, Jessie looks so good!" Simon thought to himself. He'd coveted Jessie from the moment he laid eyes on her. He'd bedded some of the wives around the office, and he'd made a few passes at Jessie. She'd never shown any interest.

But now he had her! He was going to fuck her! He was going to fuck pretty, sexy Jessie! He was going to fuck Ollie's wife!

Simon was going to take his time too. Roman said he could take as much time as he wanted. And that's what he was going to do. If this was his one and only time with Jessie, then he was going to enjoy her. He was going to enjoy her sexy body.

As agreed beforehand with Roman, Simon got onto the bed, on his knees. Roman wanted to dick around Ollie some before the action really got started, and Simon was all for that.

"Jessie, get on your knees," Roman said. When she was on her knees and facing Simon, he said, "DK, take Jessie's hands and put them on your chest. Jessie, caress his arms and chest."

As Jessie began to caress Simon, Roman said "What do you think?"

"He's got a nice body," Jessie said as she ran her fingers over Simon's biceps, pecs and abs. Simon wasn't ripped like Roman, but he played sports and worked out almost every day. His body was hard and well defined.

"Better body than Ollie?" Roman asked with a grin at Simon.

"He's more muscular than Ollie," Jessie said.

"So DK's body is better than Ollie's?" Roman asked.

"Well, yeah," Jessie said as she continued to caress Simon's muscular chest and arms. Her breathing was heavier now as she caressed Simon's hard, sexy body.

Simon was already hard, but his cock jerked as he listened to Jessie unfavorably compare her husband to him. "That's another fuck you, Ollie boy," Simon thought to himself.

"Reach down. Put your hands around DK's cock," Roman said.

Jessie did as Roman said. As her soft hands wrapped around his cock, Simon excitedly thought, "Jessie is holding my cock! She's holding my cock!"

"Is DK bigger than Ollie?" Roman asked.

"Why are we talking about Ollie so much?" Jessie asked.

With a grin in his voice, Roman said "It's fun dicking around with Metro Ollie. I know you get off on it too."

Jessie's cheeks turned even redder. It was true, it did excite her to talk about her husband this way. She didn't know why, and she hadn't felt this way when they first started playing the game. Maybe she had evolved, because Ollie himself liked her to compare him to other men. Somehow, that desire in her husband to be humiliated had sexualized itself in her, so that it also excited her to humiliate him.

"Yes, DK is bigger than Ollie," Jessie said as she slowly stroked Simon's cock.

"Shit, fuck!" Simon moaned as Jessie compared Ollie to him again. This was even better than he thought it would be!

"Okay, that's enough making fun of Jessie's husband," Roman said with a laugh. "Go ahead DK. Enjoy her. Take as much time as you want."

Simon didn't have to be asked twice. Immediately he wrapped his arms around Jessie's neck and kissed her. God her lips were so soft! He wanted all of her, including her sexy lips. When Jessie finally found out who he was, he wanted her to know she'd intimately kissed him too, not just given him her pussy.

And Jessie didn't disappoint. She kissed him back. She even parted her lips, inviting him to push in his tongue, which he did. Simon had been concerned that Jessie would be a cold fish, but she seemed to be as into it as him. The slut. He always knew she was a slut.

Simon roamed his hands over Jessie's body as they made out. God she was tight! So different from his wife Stacy, who still hadn't lost the weight she put on from her last childbirth. Where Jessie was firm, Stacy had rolls.

And Jessie's skin was so soft. Soft like a baby's.

Simon finally pulled away from Jessie's lips. He was panting. He was glad to see she was panting too.

"You're a good kisser," Jessie said between pants. Simon grinned, and glanced over at Roman. He was grinning too. He seemed happy that Jessie was responding so well to her husband's rival at work.

"Take off your bra," Simon said. He used a deeper voice, and was pretty certain she wouldn't be able to recognize him.

Jessie reached back. She unsnapped her bra. She slid the bra slid off her arms, and dropped it on the floor next to the bed.

Simon's eyes were glued to Jessie's breasts. They were perfect! Small, but perfect! His wife had big tits but they had never been perky like Jessie's. Now with age and after breast feeding, her breasts had a noticeable sag.

There was no sag to Jessie's breasts. They were perfect mounds with upturned nipples.

"You have very nice breasts," Simon said with his deeper voice as he cupped and fondled Jessie's breasts.

"Thank you," Jessie said, her cheeks getting flushed. Simon grinned. The slut liked having her tits played with.

After groping her breasts for long minutes, Simon said, "Lay down."

Once Jessie was on her back, he rubbed his hands up and down Jessie's legs. He had lusted over her legs for years. And now he was touching them! And seeing her in thigh high stockings, and stiletto high heels! God he felt like his cock was going to explode!

Simon curled his fingers into Jessie's g-string and pulled it down her long, luscious legs. He brought them to his nose. They were wet and smelled wonderful. He threw the g-string to the side of the bed. He intended to keep them as a souvenir.

Then Simon ogled her pussy. He moaned at her pretty pussy, especially when he saw she was completely bare of any pubic hair.

"Open your legs," Simon told her.

Jessie parted her legs slightly.

"Wider," he said.

Jessie opened her legs more. Now Simon had a clear view of her pussy. "Oh god," he thought. "Her pussy looks so sweet. So ripe."

Simon hadn't planned to go down on her, but now seeing her pretty pussy, he had to taste her. So he lowered his head and began eating her.

Simon licked Jessie's pussy for long minutes, until she was moaning and writhing on the bed. She was clutching the sheets and he sensed she was close to cumming. But he didn't want her to cum this way, so he stopped. He said, "You taste really good."

"My husband thinks so too," she said.

"Does he go down on you?" Simon asked, curious.

"Yes."

"Is he good?" Simon asked.

"He's really good," Jessie said. Then after a moment, she hesitantly added, "You're really good too. Maybe even better."

Simon grinned. It got him so hot the way Jessie was betraying Ollie, and not to a stranger as she thought, but to a man Ollie worked with. Simon looked over to Roman and saw that he was doing his best not to break out laughing.

Simon moved up between Jessie's legs. His cock was in his hand, guiding it to Jessie's pussy.

This was it! He was finally going to sink his cock into sweet, pretty Jessie!

He was finally going to fuck Ollie's wife!

Simon ran his cockhead up and down between Jessie's pussy lips. He grinned when Jessie moaned.

"Do you want me to fuck you?" he asked as he continued to rub her slit with his big cockhead.

"Yesssss," Jessie lustfully hissed.

"Beg me," Simon said.

"Please fuck me," Jessie begged desperately.

This was the best day of Simon's life! Pretty, sexy Jessie was begging him to fuck her!

Simon pressed his cock between Jessie's lips. Then he pushed in hard, penetrating her.

"Oh fuck you're tight!" Simon groaned as he sunk half his cock into her. And she was! So much tighter than his wife Stacy! And smoother too, like silk around his cock!

Jessie clenched her teeth as Simon pushed more of his cock into her. "You're really big," she gasped. "Not as big as Romes. But bigger than my husband. So much bigger."

"Oh god fuck!" Simon moaned. He loved the way Jessie was demeaning Ollie! Both by giving her pussy to him, and by humbling him with her words. He loved it!

Simon began fucking Jessie. As he did, he caressed her body, especially her tits and ass. He also leaned down and kissed her.

Jessie kissed him back, and moaned into his mouth. Simon's cock felt really good inside her. It had a curve to it, and his cockhead was really fat. On top of that, Simon really knew how to fuck. Jessie found her body quickly responding to him.

"Romes, he's gonna make me cum," she warned, desperation in her voice.

"Do you want him to make you cum?" Roman asked.

"Yesssss!" Jessie begged.

"It's okay Jessie," Roman told her. "You can cum on DK's cock."

Jessie wasn't going to question Roman. Now that she had his permission, she gave into it, she allowed herself to fully enjoy the fuck, because the man she knew as DK was really freaking good. She could tell he was a very experienced lover. He had a big cock and knew how to use it. And his hands were very skilled with touching a girl and turning her on. Roman was the best, but this man was easily the second best lover in her life.

Simon put Jessie's legs on his shoulders, loving the way the silky nylon of her thigh highs felt against his bare skin. He began fucking her harder, feeling his orgasm approaching, but he wanted to make Jessie came first.

And moments later she was cumming. Jessie arched her back and cried out as she went over the edge, her pretty stockinged toes curling in the shiny black *So Kate* high heels as orgasmic pleasure flooded her body.

Knowing Jessie had cum, Simon let himself go. He pushed hard into her pussy as he came, banging her hard over and over, each thrust sending millions of his fertile seeds into Jessie's unprotected, fertile womb.

To emphasize the point, Roman said, "Hey DK. Jessie's not on birth control. You may have just put a baby in her."

"Are you fucking serious?" DK said, amazed. He looked down at Jessie's pretty face. She was panting as she came down from her orgasm.

She looked so beautiful at that moment. So perfect. And the fact he might have just impregnated her got him fired up.

He leaned down and began kissing her and fondling her body. He had never pulled out, and he felt his erection returning. He wanted to fuck her again, cum in her again and have another chance to impregnant the cheating slut. That would be the ultimate fuck you to Ollie.

Jessie responded to Simon's kisses and caresses. He was a really awesome lover, and he knew how to work a girl's body and give her pleasure.

Soon they were fucking again. It took longer this time, and by the time they were both close, their bodies were covered with sweat.

"Oh god, oh god, you're gonna freaking make me cum again!" Jessie moaned. She was close to another orgasm, and Simon knew it. He was close too.

"Does Ollie make you cum?" Simon asked, getting into the spirit of humiliating his rival.

"God no, his dick's too small to make me cum!" Jessie said lustfully. "But you're so big, you feel so good inside me! Oh god, you're gonna make me cum again!"

At the point of no return, Simon pulled off Jessie's eye mask. It took Jessie a moment for her eyes to focus, but then she saw him. Her eyes went wide with recognition.

"Yes Jessie. It me, Simon," Simon said in his normal voice, grinning lecherously at her.

"No, no!" Jessie screamed, trying to squirm away.

But Simon was too strong. And his cock was too deep inside her. And they both were too far along anyway.

"I made you cum once!" Simon tauntingly said. "I'm about to make you cum again!"

"No Simon, get off me!" Jessie said, trying to get away from him. But now he had her hands pinned above her head.

"You're gonna be kissing me when you cum on my cock!" Simon said with a cruel smile. Then before she could react, Simon leaned down and kissed Jessie. She tried to twist her head away from his lips but he was too insistent. Soon she felt his tongue in her mouth as he continued to pound her pussy with his big cock.

Jessie's body was betraying her. She didn't want this man to make her cum, but his cock felt too good inside her, and he was too skilled a lover. There was no way she could stop it, Simon was going to make her cum.

"I'm about there, Jessie," Simon warned with labored breathing. "Your pussy feels so good. Your pussy is so fucking tight. So much better than Stacy's."

"Pull out Simon!" Jessie begged desperately. "Please don't cum inside me!"

"No way Jessie," Simon said. He was panting now, on the brink of his climax. "You're gonna take all my seed. Then I'm gonna laugh in Ollie's face when you're fat with my baby."

"Here it comes, Jessie!" Simon roared as he went over the edge. He tightly gripped her hips to penetrate her as deeply as possible. Then he thrusted hard into her, again and again, each time shooting potent baby making seed into her unprotected fertile pussy, and yelling "Take it! Take it! Take it!"

Simon's violent pounding sent Jessie over the edge. She cried out and arched her back as she came. As her body spasmed with orgasmic pleasure, Simon locked his lips over hers, kissing her. In the midst of an incredible orgasm, Jessie instinctively wrapped her arms around Simon's neck, passionately kissing him back, betraying her husband once more in the most devastating way.

⟶⬤⟵

"What the fuck! Are you freaking crazy!" Jessie screamed after Simon was gone. She was hurriedly dressing.

"Jessie, come on, it's just fun," Roman said, laughing.

"Simon works with Ollie! You know that! I told you we had to be discreet! And now you just outed us!"

"Don't worry," Roman said dismissively, the laugh still in his voice. "Simon promised he won't say anything. Remember, if he says something, he fucks himself over because then Stacy will find out."

"You still had no right! No right!"

"Jessie will you calm down?" Roman said, a big grin on his face. "We're just playing. Fucking around with Ollie some. I know that gets you hot too. I can tell."

"Fuck you Roman!" Jessie screamed, and she slapped his face. Then she stormed out of his house.

CHAPTER 17

Their fears became reality. Simon blabbed to everyone at work he fucked Jessie.

Unbeknownst to Roman, he had positioned his iPhone to video it all. So he had proof, and Ollie and Jessie had no way of denying it.

Ollie was completely humiliated and ruined. There was no way he could continue working at the firm, so by the end of the week he tendered his resignation. He also couldn't land a job anywhere in New York City, as Simon's video went viral. It was everywhere, and Simon was proud of it. After all, he had gotten a super-hot girl off twice with his cock, and the video proved that she loved fucking him.

Simon lied to Roman about keeping quiet. He didn't care if Stacy found out, because he planned to divorce her anyway. She was getting older and not ageing well, with fading looks and sagging tits. He wanted to replace her with a girl who was younger and prettier. Within a month after fucking Jessie, Simon deserted his wife and children and filed for divorce.

<hr>

A few days after Ollie lost his job, Jessie went to see Roman at his gym. She found him in his office.

"I have to stop seeing you," she told him.

"Why?"

"Why?" Jessie said incredulously. "Because you freaking ruined my husband's career!"

"Jessie, calm down," Roman said dismissively.

"Stop telling me to calm down!" she angrily yelled.

Roman pulled Jessie into his arms. "Look, okay, I fucked up," he admitted. "Really fucked up. But we've got a connection. Something special. I love you. And I think you love me."

"I don't love you," Jessie said, but her tone was softer, and the anger was subsiding. Roman sensed her resolve was weakening.

Roman hugged her tighter. He said, "I know I fucked up. I'm really sorry. I know I hurt Ollie. But he'll land on his feet. He's super smart, and nice. People like that always come out okay."

"I'm so ashamed after that video," Jessie said, tears welling up in her eyes. She was no longer trying to pull away. "How could I have been so horrible to him? I hate myself right now."

"It's not just you, Jessie," Roman said soothingly. "We were both horrible to him. I took it too far, and he got hurt. I'm make it right Jessie. I'll do whatever I can to help Ollie out."

Jessie sobbed into Roman's chest as he held her and whispered soothing nothings into her ear.

After a few moments, Roman lifted Jessie face so she was looking at him. Then he kissed the tears away.

Eventually his lips moved to hers and he kissed her.

"No Roman, we can't," Jessie said, but her attempts to pull away were half-hearted.

"We love each other Jessie," Roman said as he kissed her again. "We're perfect for each other."

Soon they were passionately kissing. And then they were naked and on his sofa. Roman was inside Jessie. Their sex was gentle and loving. They kissed as they made love.

They both came at the same time. Roman kissed Jessie all over her pretty face as she panted, recovering from her orgasm.

"Please get off me," Jessie said.

"Jessie ...."

"Please Roman, get off me," she said again.

Roman pulled out of Jessie's pussy. The huge load of sperm he just shot inside her immediately began seeping from her pussy.

"You don't call me Romes anymore?" Roman asked.

"We can't do this again," Jessie said as she began putting her clothes back on. She was sad. Her voice was full of emotion.

"You can't mean that. I love you. I want to marry you."

"What?" Jessie said, shocked.

"Please marry me Jessie," Roman implored.

"Don't ask me that Roman," Jessie asked, shaking her head with tears in her eyes. "I can't do that to Ollie. I've already hurt him too much. I can't leave him."

"Ollie's a really nice guy. A great guy," Roman said. "But this is your life, Jessie. Our lives. You can't be unhappy the rest of your life just because you feel like you owe him something."

"I never said that," Jessie said. She was sobbing now. "I've got to go."

"You're really breaking up with me?" Roman asked. Now his voice was full of emotion. Tears began falling down his cheeks.

"I can't hurt Ollie!" Jessie said between sobs.

"But what about me?" Roman asked. He was crying too. "If you break up with me, you're hurting me!"

"I've got to go Roman," Jessie said, turning away.

"No Jessie you can't!" Roman said, reaching for her hand but she pulled it away.

"I've got to go Roman," Jessie said again. With a sob, she said, "I can't see you again."

With tears in his eyes, Roman croaked out, "Jessie ... how can you do this to me?"

With another sob and tears running down her face, Jessie ran out of the room.

EPILOGUE

The following months were hard for Ollie and Jessie.

Jessie cried all the time. Breaking up with Roman was really hard for her. They'd shared so many things together, and she cared for him deeply. Suddenly not having him in her life anymore was like losing a part of herself. Many times during the day, she'd curl into a ball and sob uncontrollably as she mourned the end of her relationship with Roman.

Jessie knew it hurt Ollie to see her this way. But there was nothing she could do. More than once, she sobbed, "I'm sorry Ollie. But I just have to feel this way until I don't feel this way anymore."

Ollie thought about leaving Jessie. Not that he wanted to. He didn't.

But she was so unhappy. He began thinking she'd be happier with Roman instead of him. He began thinking that the best thing he could do for Jessie was to get out of the way so she could be with Roman.

When he mentioned this, Jessie broke down in sobs. "I picked you Ollie!" she cried. "You can't leave me after all this! I picked you!"

Eventually things began to get better. Jessie cried less and less, until one day she didn't cry at all. And there were some days she didn't think about Roman, not even once.

Ollie became a financial advisor. Jessie's Broadway musical ended. She didn't try to get another gig. And she didn't want to go back to her old job, because she hated it. So instead, Jessie worked as Ollie's office manager, and helped with his marketing. Eventually they got enough clients to make ends meet.

Ollie and Jessie's sex life was almost non-existent. By unspoken agreement, they made sure to have sex at least once a week. But their sex wasn't passionate or exciting. They were just going through the motions.

Maybe they'd been through too much. Experienced too much. Maybe they needed something more to spice up their sex life.

They began talking about adding another person. Another man. And suddenly, with that pillow talk, their sex life became exciting again.

For months it was just pillow talk. Then they began talking about whether they should go from fantasy to reality. But they knew the dangers and risks. Was the thrill of adding another man to their relationship worth the heartache that would eventually result?

One day in the local newspaper, Jessie saw an article about their old church. It was an interview with Pastor John, about his decision to be sexually celibate even though the church didn't require it.

"I guess he decided to stay celibate after all," Jessie said.

"What?" Ollie asked, not understanding.

Jessie told her husband about the conversation she had with Pastor John months ago, when he told her he missed sex with girls.

"It must be important to him to stay celibate," Ollie said.

"Yeah, I guess," Jessie said. She was looking at the picture of Pastor John in the article.

Ollie saw how closely Jessie was studying the picture. "Do you think he's handsome?" he asked.

"I mean, yeah," Jessie said with a laugh. "I guess. Sure."

Ollie felt a tingling in his loins. He said, "You know, maybe he's still celibate, because he hasn't found the right girl to not be celibate with."

Jessie looked at her husband. She said, "Are you freaking thinking what I think you're thinking?"

"It would be wicked," Ollie said with a grin.

"We'd go to hell for sure," Jessie said with a laugh.

Then Jessie said, "Ollie, baby, are you serious?"

The married couple looked at each other for long moments. Then Jessie said, "He did say I could call him if I needed someone to talk to."

"You could say you need to confess," Ollie said with a teasing grin.

"Oh? About what?" Jessie said grinning back.

"You could say you're still feeling guilty about the video," Ollie suggested.

"Oh my god!" Jessie said with another laugh.

"I've got an idea," Ollie said. He took Jessie phone and pushed some keys. Then with a big grin, he handed the phone back to Jessie.

"What did you just do?" Jessie warily asked.

"I sent a text to Pastor John. From you," Ollie said. "You just told him you're still feeling guilty about the video, and wanted to talk to him about it. And I included a link to the video."

Jessie's eyes got wide. "Oh my god Ollie, you did not!" she said.

Then they both turned as Jessie's phone began to ring. The caller ID said: Pastor John.

Don't miss out!

Visit the website below and you can sign up to receive emails whenever Pete Andrews publishes a new book. There's no charge and no obligation.

https://books2read.com/r/B-A-KWSAB-WJVOC

BOOKS 2 READ

Connecting independent readers to independent writers.

www.ingramcontent.com/pod-product-compliance
Lightning Source LLC
Chambersburg PA
CBHW051226160726

47994CB00002B/761